MW00779385

THE GIRL IN THE BASEMENT

THE GIRL IN THE BASEMENT

Ray Garton

OPEN ROAD

INTEGRATED MEDIA

NEW YORK

All rights reserved, including without limitation the right to reproduce this book or any portion thereof in any form or by any means, whether electronic or mechanical, now known or hereinafter invented, without the express written permission of the publisher.

This is a work of fiction. Names, characters, places, events, and incidents either are the product of the author's imagination or are used fictitiously. Any resemblance to actual persons, living or dead, businesses, companies, events, or locales is entirely coincidental.

Copyright © 2004 by Ray Garton

ISBN 978-1-4976-4264-5

This edition published in 2014 by Open Road Integrated Media, Inc.
345 Hudson Street
New York, NY 10014
www.openroadmedia.com

For Dawn

From the Journal of Ryan Kettering

Foster care is like playing Russian Roulette. Sometimes the hammer clicks and you're fine, and sometimes you take a bullet to the brain.

Like the fat guy who beat his wife and used to come into my room late at night and make me do things. That was taking a bullet to the brain. I wasn't there very long, though, because some other kid ratted on the guy and all the foster kids were taken out of their house.

Or those really religious people who made us pray all the time. The man used to beat us with the belt. They were always playing this religious music on the stereo, organ music a lot of the time, like something from an old horror movie. Not CDs or tapes, either, but old vinyl records with lots of scratches and pops on them. That place was so depressing. Another bullet.

The place I'm in now is pretty nice, though. The hammer clicked this time. It's a big house, it's fucking huge and rambling and stands on a plot of land off Fig Tree Lane between two old oak trees. Two stories tall with an attic so big, it's been converted into a roomy bedroom—that's where Lyssa, Candy, and Nicole sleep—and a basement big enough to hold a bedroom and a large rec room. The house has central air conditioning, which is nice in Shasta County's blistering summers, like the one we're having now, and there's a big back yard with a nice concrete swimming pool. The woman's name is Marie. She's short and really fat, and she always wears her hair pulled back in a bun. She smiles all the time, even when she's angry. It's kind of creepy sometimes. But she's okay. It seems like she's always rushing around in the kitchen. Her husband's name is Hank, and he's this tall, broad-shouldered guy with only one arm. He lost his right arm in some kind of machine. He used to work in a factory. Now he's got this plastic arm with these metal hooks he can open and close on the end of it. He's got a gut on him, from all the beer he drinks. He sits and watches TV a lot, while she's bustling around in the kitchen. Meanwhile, they've got us working around the house most of the time. Marie keeps the girls busy with cleaning the house and doing laundry and any other thing she can think of, and he keeps us boys—along with me, there's Gary and Keith—busy doing yardwork and working on the house. The only one who doesn't do any work is the girl in the basement. But they're okay, Hank and Marie. They're old, in their fifties, I think, but they're okay.

It seems the only time Marie leaves the kitchen is to take care of Maddy. It's short for Madrigal—what the hell kind of name is Madrigal? Maddy stays in the bedroom in the basement. I mean, she really stays there—the only time she comes out is once a day when Marie walks her out the back door and around the backyard a few times. Sometimes, Marie asks one of the girls to help her with Maddy. Never the boys. We only see Maddy if we happen to be around when Marie takes her out for her walk.

I was making out with Lyssa in the rec room awhile ago. We've been meeting there at one or two in the morning, after everyone's asleep. We're the newest kids in the home and there was an instant attraction between us when I came three months ago. She'd only been here a month herself back then. She brought a blanket and we stretched out on the couch in the rec room and put the blanket over us. I always use a rubber. I'm fifteen years old and I got a summer job bagging groceries and lifting things at Kent's Market down the street, and I don't need a pregnant girl staring me in the face.

Lyssa is amazingly hot. She's got long black hair and this pale milky skin that I just have to touch when I look at it. She has the kind of body that makes guys bite their hands.

Afterward, we just lay there talking in whispers and she told me she'd helped Marie with Maddy a couple times, most recently the day before.

"Maddy doesn't dress herself," Lyssa said, "so I helped Marie change her clothes."

"What's she like?" I asked.

"Somethin's wrong with that girl," Lyssa said.

I said that she looked fat, and she did. I'd seen Maddy a few times. She looked big and lumbering, with a fat face and narrow piggy eyes, and a flat piggy nose.

"She's big for her age," Lyssa said. "Marie says she's nine, but she's so big-boned and fat. But that's not what's wrong with her."

"Then what is?"

"I ... don't know for sure. Sometimes Maddy looks right through you, like you're not there. Then other times, she looks at you like she can see inside you, like she can see your most secret thoughts. Sometimes she talks and she sounds like a little girl. And sometimes she says things ... really strange things ... and her voice is deep and almost sounds like a man's. Sometimes she talks nonsense, and it sounds like she's speaking another language."

"What kind of strange things does she say?"

"Today, she looked at me, she looked into my eyes and looked deep, Ryan, she saw inside me, I swear, and her voice went deep when she said, 'Sadness will be your constant companion through life, girl.'" Lyssa turned her head to me. It was dark and I couldn't see her face, but there was something scared about the way she moved her head. "That scared me, Ryan. It really scared me. The way she said 'girl,' it ... it sounded like an adult talking to me, it really did, like someone ... old. Really old. And what if she's right? I mean, what if she looked inside me and saw that?"

I chuckled. "Cut it out. She's a retarded girl."

"I don't think she's retarded."

"All you have to do is look at her to see she's retarded. She's got that ... well, that look to her, you know?"

"But what if she's right, Ryan? What if she's right? That girl really gives me the creeps."

Something about Maddy had made Lyssa think it was at least possible that the girl wasn't just rattling off whatever popped into her head. Something about Maddy had frightened Lyssa deeply.

That intrigues me. From what I've seen, Maddy's just a lumbering little retarded girl who's not so little, a sad sight, the kind of child who makes you click your tongue and think, *That's too bad.* But she'd scared the hell out of Lyssa. Clearly there's more to this Maddy girl than I thought. I haven't been told to stay away from Maddy, but it's been made clear to me that she lives separately and is not a part of the general population of the house. It seems kind of sad that she's kept down in the basement by herself all the time. I don't see any reason why I shouldn't stop by and pay Maddy a visit tomorrow.

ONE

Elliott Granger pushed his walker to the open front door and looked through the security door as Ryan Kettering finished mowing his front lawn. The lawn had been tall and bushy with weeds before Ryan came over and offered to mow it. Elliott knew Marie next door had sent him over—she had been taking good care of him while he was down with the hip.

While Elliott wasn't too sure about the other two boys in the group home next door, he thought Ryan was a good kid. Marie had told him Ryan's mother was a drug addict who lived on the street half the time, going from fix to fix. No one knew who his father was, but Marie said Ryan had expressed no interest in finding out.

Ryan was very guarded. When he first met the boy, Elliott sensed the walls he threw up. Then one day, Ryan learned Elliott was a writer and expressed an interest in his work. Elliott gave him copies of a couple young adult thrillers he'd written. After reading them, Ryan had discussed them with him. He'd expressed an interest in writing and Elliott had told him to keep a journal, write down his thoughts and experiences. Elliott got the feeling the boy was so guarded because his feelings were just beneath the surface, raw and vulnerable to hurt. He knew how therapeutic it could be to write about those feelings, to drain them on the page.

Elliott Granger was a writer of horror fiction. It was the only thing he'd ever wanted to do with his life since he was eight years old. He had no problem with the fact that he was a horror writer, but so many others seemed to that he hesitated to admit it when asked, "What do you do?"

"I write for a living."

"Oh, what do you write?"

"Novels mostly, but a short story now and then."

"What kind of novels?"

At this point, Elliott usually had not spent enough time with the person to have any idea how they would feel about his being a horror writer, so he'd have to make a snap personality judgment, or just play it safe and say, "Thrillers, mysteries."

"What kind of thrillers?"

He usually gave in quickly and confessed the truth. "Horror, actually, I write horror novels."

Their true reaction did not come right away, it came a little later. First, they had to say the inevitable: "You mean, like Stephen King?"

While they did the same thing for a living, Elliott's advances were not even in the same galaxy as Stephen King's. This was always the first thing discussed by everyone, man, woman, and child, without exception, when they learned that Elliott wrote horror novels.

"Wow, I betcha you'd like to get some of *his* royalties by mistake, wouldn'tcha?"

"You could probably live well off his interest, couldn't you?"

"You ever think of writing a book the way *he* does it?"

"Do you *know* Stephen King?"

Sometimes, Elliott felt like saying, "Of course, he comes to *all* the meetings," but he never had because it was snide and unpleasant, and he tried never to be snide and unpleasant to potential readers. He had, however, tried two different answers to the question. When, in response to, "Do you *know* Stephen King?" he said that he'd *met* Stephen King, people were always friendlier to him than they were when he was honest and said no, he did not know King. So he had King to thank for that.

Then, once all the frivolity about Stephen King was over, it started to set in—they realized that this guy actually *thought that stuff up*, and they began to get suspicious. And he didn't even do it for millions of dollars, like King—it was common knowledge in town that he lived in his parents' house because he was flat broke and was having trouble selling a new novel, when he could be making perfectly good money at a perfectly normal job.

"Where do you get your ideas?"

"How do you *think* of such things?"

"Do you just sit around and think about *horror* all the time?"

"*Why* do you write *horror*?"

And that was about the time he usually lost them, when he

couldn't come up with a satisfactory answer for them—and who could? He preferred King's response: "What makes you think I've got a choice?" But that never made anybody feel any better.

Ryan turned off the mower and rolled it into the garage. It was a few minutes after ten in the morning, but it was already hot. Ryan was sweaty as he came out of the garage and headed for the front door. He wore an X-Men T-shirt, a pair of denim cut-offs, and old sneakers. He was a slender-muscled boy with a thick head of blond hair.

"Come on inside," Elliott said as he backed away from the door.

Ryan came inside.

"Here, take this," Elliott said, handing him a ten dollar bill.

"Oh, no, you don't have to pay me, Marie told me to just come over and—"

"I know, I know, but go ahead and take it, anyway."

"But I didn't even do the back lawn."

"So you can do the back lawn tomorrow morning."

Ryan hesitated, but finally took the ten and stuffed it into his pocket. "Thanks, Mr. Granger. By the way, I took your advice."

"What advice was that?"

"I started a journal."

"Hey, that's good. Now, if you ever decide to try writing a short story, let me know. I want to read it."

"Okay. I might take you up on that." Ryan shrugged. "Well, I guess I'll go. But I'll come back tomorrow morning and do the back lawn, I promise. It's getting hotter fast out there."

"That sounds good, Ryan. Give Marie my best."

On his way out, Ryan said, "I think she's cooking something for you."

"She's always cooking something for me. I don't know what I would've done without her."

Marie Preston had made sure he was well fed and cared for the last few months. In fact, he'd put on a few pounds eating her food. The pain from the osteonecrosis had been excruciating and he'd been unable to walk without crutches before surgery. It had hurt too much to write, and not writing had made him feel like a useless vegetable. His right hip had been replaced with a prosthesis. He'd had the surgery only a couple months ago and was recovering.

He hobbled with the walker back down the hall to his office and seated himself—he winced at the pain in his hip when he sat—at the computer on his desk. His cup of coffee was next to the keyboard. He read the morning's headline stories in a number of different newspapers while Diane Krall played on his stereo.

Elliott and his brother and sister had grown up in the four-bedroom ranch-style house in which he now lived alone. When his father died, his mother had used the money from his life insurance to buy a double-wide mobile home in a park across Airport Road from Fig Tree Lane, just north of Kent's Market. The house was too big for her to keep clean, but she didn't have the heart to sell it. That had been four years ago, about the time Elliott and his wife Irene were getting a divorce, and Elliott had moved into the house.

"Stay as long as you like," his mother had told him. "Think of the place as yours."

He always had. The house was home.

His brother Mike was a twice-married veterinarian with a son in Red Bluff and his sister Angie lived with her therapist husband and their two kids in Sacramento. Elliott and Irene had an eight-year-old daughter, Lizzy, who lived with her mother. Elliott saw her every other weekend, although Irene had brought her by more often since he'd been down with his hip, and he'd been grateful for that—Irene even had made an effort to be civil. On the corner of Elliott's desk stood a stuffed Opus the penguin—it belonged to Lizzy, and she had left it to take care of him while he was recovering.

He was ready to get to work when he drank the last of his coffee. He reached for the single crutch leaning against the wall by the desk. When he had to carry a drink, he walked with one crutch, although it was more painful than walking with two, or using the walker. He was halfway down the hall when the doorbell rang.

"Coming!" he called. He opened the door and found Marie standing there holding a pie in both hands, smiling. He pushed open the security door. "Uh-oh, looks like you've been baking, Marie."

"The girls and I went blackberry picking down by the river early this morning," she said as she came in. "I made an extra pie for you, Elliott."

"It looks delicious, Marie."

She took the pie to the kitchen and set it on the counter. "Is there anything I can do for you while I'm here?"

"No, thanks, Marie. I'm good for now. I can't thank you enough."

"I see Ryan mowed your lawn for you."

"Yes, he did. I like Ryan. He's a good kid."

"Yes, he is. His mother is coming to see him this morning."

"Really? He didn't say anything about it when he was here."

"He just found out himself. She only called a few minutes ago." Her smile faltered. "Sometimes I think her visits do more harm than good to that boy. He always seems so unhappy after she goes."

"How is she?" Elliott asked. "I mean, is she off the drugs?"

"She's better sometimes than others, but she just doesn't seem able to shake the drugs for long. They've really got their hooks in her."

"That's too bad," Elliott said.

He thanked her again and she reminded him to call her if he needed help with anything, then she left. He felt bad for Ryan. What must it be like to know your own mother can't take care of you because her addiction to drugs takes precedence in her life?

He got a fresh cup of coffee and went back to his office to work.

TWO

Ryan did not want to see Phyllis—that was his mother's name, and that's how he thought of her, as Phyllis, not Mom—but no one ever asked him if he *wanted* to see her or not. She just showed up once in awhile. She usually looked worse each time, and this time was no exception.

Marie put them at the dining room table together—Phyllis at the end and Ryan on the side, with only the table's corner between them—with iced tea and a slice of blackberry pie each.

"How ya doin', honey?" Phyllis asked.

"I'm fine," he said, staring at his pie.

"Well, look at me, sweetheart." She reached over and hooked a finger under his chin, lifted his head. "I haven't seen you in—how long's it been?"

"Since Christmas."

"Has it been that long?"

She could not hold still. She jittered and fidgeted at the table as if she were about to come out of her skin. Her pale, rough face seemed to be collapsing—her top front four teeth were gone, and most of her bottom teeth as well, and her lips and cheeks sank into her face, and her temples were twin indentations flanking her brow, giving her face a skull-like appearance. Her nose, pierced in the left nostril, was always runny and sniffly, her eyes always red. There were dark grey half-moons beneath her eyes, and her blonde hair was pulled back in a ponytail and looked unwashed. She was skinny and all bones. She wore a red halter-top and a pair of jeans that looked too big on her, cinched tight at her waist with a thin, worn red belt. Her arms and shoulders were pale, with a yellowish hue, small dark bruises here and there. The old track marks on her arms were ugly, but she made no effort to hide them. Her hands never stopped moving. They touched her hair, her face, fumbled with each other, fed pie into her mouth, reached across the table to squeeze Ryan's hands. They were like spiders on the ends of her arms, crawling here and there and all around.

"I thought I'd come by and let you know I got me a place," she said. "You know the Lazy Z Ranch, that little motel off Highway 273 on Spring Gulch Road?"

Ryan knew the place. It was a run-down flea-pit with little bungalows arranged in a U shape with a small courtyard in the center and a pool off to one side. The pool had been empty for as long as he could remember. The Lazy Z was a motel, but people lived there—drug addicts and alcoholics who couldn't get apartments. People like Phyllis. People like his mother.

"Yeah, I know where it is," he said.

"Well, I got me one a them little bungalows now," she said as she reached across the table and squeezed his hand. She took a bite of her pie and talked while she chewed. "You can ride your bike over there and see me sometime, couldn'tcha?"

He shrugged. "It's on the other side of town."

"Oh, I know, but you ride your bike everywhere, don'tcha, honey? I'd like to introduce you t'all my friends over there. I want 'em to see what a handsome son I got. Would you like that? To come and meet my friends?"

I'd rather eat my own lips, he thought, but said, "Yeah, sure. Maybe sometime."

"I'm clean, y'know," she said.

Yeah, right, he thought.

"Been clean for sixteen days now," she said.

He didn't believe a word of it.

"Aren't you proud of me?"

He nodded. "Yeah. Yeah."

She asked about his job, how he liked living with the Prestons. Ryan answered the questions, all the while trying not to look at her. Her eyes were set so deep in her skull, and there was something about them that he didn't like—a hunger, a desperate need. Her eyes looked like they wanted to suck him dry, to drain him of his energy, his youth, his health.

"Well, I gotta go," she said after she finished the pie. "I borrowed a friend's car and I promised her I'd have it back by eleven. You wanna ride with me over to the Lazy Z? I could prob'ly get you a ride back."

"I've gotta go to work soon," Ryan said. He was relieved to be able to say it.

"Oh, well, we don't wantcha to miss work."

She made a big deal of hugging and kissing him, like she always did. He'd decided some time ago that the visits were something she probably did for herself. Whenever she started thinking about him and suffered pangs of guilt, she made a quick visit and touched him a lot and gave him a big hug and kiss and convinced herself she was a loving mother. He certainly hoped the visits weren't for *his* benefit, because if so, they didn't work.

After she left, he went to the bedroom he shared with Gary and Keith. A wall had been knocked out to combine two smallish rooms into a larger one. There were two sets of bunk beds on opposite sides of the room. The boys had put up posters of swimsuit models and rock bands.

Ryan had the bottom bunk on the eastern wall—the top bunk was unoccupied—and he sat on the edge of his bed and put his elbows on his thighs, his face in his hands. Visiting with his mother always tired him out. It was exhausting, the way she constantly moved and twitched and jittered, the way she kept touching him and squeezing, squeezing, as if she were trying to milk something out of him—love, or acceptance, or—

Maybe forgiveness, Ryan thought. But he doubted it.

Gary and Keith came into the room laughing. Gary punched Ryan in the shoulder and said, "Keith and the old man were just playing ping pong down in the rec room and Keith beat him three times in a row. It's drivin' the old man crazy."

"He couldn't take it anymore," Keith said, "so now we gotta go weed the garden."

"You toasted him," Gary said, holding up a hand, and Keith high-fived him.

Gary was annoying at times. He was overly enthusiastic about everything, filled with nervous energy, a little twitchy. He was seventeen years old—less than a year left in this branch of the system for Gary—and he was the kind of guy who, if he couldn't find some trouble to get into, would invent some, and then get into it. He was short, about five feet, six inches tall, and skinny. He had a thick head of black hair and piercing blue eyes that usually looked a little too wide. He was good with cars, and had a part-time job at a garage in Anderson. There was usually grease under his nails.

Keith, fifteen, was probably the worst kind of person you possibly could have around a guy like Gary—Keith was a follower, and he followed Gary like a disciple. He was over six feet tall and ducked his head slightly in an attempt to lessen his height. He was big and doughy and clumsy with a mop of rusty hair and a mustache he was trying to grow. He cleared his throat frequently—it was more of a nervous tic than an actual clearing of his throat. He parroted everything Gary said and seemed to have no thoughts of his own. He was usually pretty quiet.

Gary and Keith changed into their oldest, rattiest jeans and a couple torn old T-shirts to work in the garden.

"How about some airhockey later on, Ryan, huh?" Gary said.

"Yeah, sure, when I get back from work. Maybe after dinner."

Ryan took a shower, then scrubbed himself dry. He put on jeans and a shortsleeve yellow shirt. On his way out, Marie stopped him.

"You okay, Ryan?" she said, smiling as always.

"Yeah, I'm fine."

"You didn't eat your pie."

"Oh, yeah, I'm sorry, I just wasn't hungry. I'll eat it later, okay?"

"I'll put it in the fridge for you. Your mom ... she didn't stay very long, did she?"

"Just long enough to eat her pie. I think she really liked it."

"You off to work now?"

"Yeah. I'll be back later."

He got on his bike and headed up Fig Tree Lane. The July sky was a brilliant blue with billowing white clouds off toward Mt. Shasta, the purple, white-spotted sleeping lady that rose up in the north. High overhead, a commercial jet the size of a mosquito left behind a tiny white trail.

He listened to the air blowing over his ears as he rode and tried not to think about Phyllis. He remembered that he'd planned to pay a visit to Maddy in the basement today. He regretted not doing it that morning, before work. He would have to try that evening.

At the end of Fig Tree, he stopped and waited for a break in the traffic on Airport Road. When it came, he crossed and rode his bike into the crowded parking lot of Kent's Market. He chained his bike to a rack on the side of the building, then went inside. He went in back and put on his green smock. Kent put him in the reefer with Karil stocking the beverage coolers. It was cold back there, and it felt good after being outside in the heat.

Ryan had been working at Kent's for two months, but Karil had just started a few days ago. She was about his age, a tall, raw-boned girl with long red hair and clusters of freckles on her cheeks.

"You're Ryan, right?" she said.

"Yeah."

"I have a terrible time remembering people's names."

He smiled. "Mine's pretty easy to remember."

They worked for awhile, then she said, "So, you ... you live in a group home, right?"

"Yeah."

"What's that like?"

"Not like everybody thinks," Ryan said with a shake of his head.

"What does everybody think?"

"I'm not sure, but people seem to freak out when they learn there's a group home in the neighborhood. I mean, jeez, it's just foster kids, not the criminally insane, you know? It's not like we're all these foaming-at-the-mouth criminals."

"Yeah. People do think that, don't they?"

"Every place I've ever lived, most of the neighbors hate the fact that there's a group home on their street or on their block. They think we're gonna rob their homes when their gone and rape their daughters at night, or something. When the fact is, I prefer to do all my raping during the day so I can see what I'm doing."

Karil turned to him with wide eyes, her full pink lips parted. She stared at him for a few long seconds, then he smiled.

"I'm kidding," he said.

"Oh," she said, and she laughed and rolled her eyes at her own gullibility. "I-I didn't think you were a rapist, really, I was just, well—"

He chuckled and said, "It's okay, you don't have to explain yourself."

"So, what happened to your parents?"

"My mom's a drug addict and I don't know who my dad is. What about yours?"

"Oh, mine? Uh, well ... my dad's a podiatrist and my mom has a little antique store in Redding. We live over in Wooded Acres." She gestured west.

"Any brothers or sisters?"

"No. I'm an only child. Which puts a lot of pressure on me. I mean, y'know, I have to be the smart one, the good looking one, the successful one, all rolled up into one."

Ryan frowned. "Aren't you putting a lot of that pressure on yourself?"

"Oh, no. You don't know my parents. Trust me. *They're* puttin' the pressure on."

Ryan might complain about this or that now and then, but he never complained about growing up without a permanent set of parents. All the people he knew who had them seemed so deeply unhappy with them.

THREE

After dinner that night, Gary reminded Ryan of their planned airhockey game. They went down to the spacious basement. The Prestons had done a pretty good job of furnishing their rec room. It had a ping pong table, an ancient airhockey table, bumper pool, a couple pinball machines, two dartboards, and an arcade PacMan. There was a couch and a couple chairs arranged around a television, and cupboards against the back wall contained shelves of DVDs to choose from. It was all wholesome family fare, nothing of interest to Ryan. But it was a place to watch the DVDs he rented. Nobody in the house was interested in the movies Ryan liked to watch, except for Gary, who was interested in everything. When he came in and found Ryan watching, say, a Japanese horror movie, Gary wanted to know who starred in it, who had produced, written, and directed it, what it was about, and whether or not it was any good. Ryan always paused the movie, listed off its credits for him, and caught him up on the plot. He didn't mind the intrusion. Gary wasn't a bad guy. He wasn't a great guy, but he wasn't a bad guy.

Ryan played airhockey with Gary for awhile and Keith watched. The girls came down a little later and Nicole said she wanted to play the winner. Ryan intentionally lost the game.

Nicole was fifteen, a heavyset girl with a pretty face, short blonde hair, and big blue eyes. She was a challenger, always challenging people to arm wrestling matches or games in the rec room or stare-downs. Ryan had never acknowledged any of her challenges—he'd just ignored them, as if she hadn't said anything at all—and for that reason, it seemed, she was comfortable talking to him. Usually when she talked to him, it was about her mother, who was in jail for prostitution. Ryan listened. He spoke up once in awhile, usually for clarification, but mostly he just listened. That was all she seemed to want and need, someone to listen.

Candy was a sixteen-year-old sex fiend. She had a voluptuous body, and she enjoyed displaying it for the boys. Marie was always telling her to go put something on. She had frizzy, shoulder-length brown hair and an hourglass figure. Tonight, she wore a tight blue bellyshirt and tight red shorts. She looked like she'd been drawn for an adult comic book. Candy had come to his bed his first night there. Three in the morning, she'd awakened him with a kiss and tried to get under the covers with him. He told her to get the hell out of his room. It was his first night, and he didn't want to get in trouble on his first night at a new place, it would get things off to a bad start, so he told her to get the hell out of his room. The next morning, he'd tried to explain his reasons to her, but she wasn't interested in them. She'd never returned to his bed, and she'd been chilly toward him ever since.

Then there was Lyssa. Ryan felt his smile stretch to its limits when he saw her come into the rec room. After he lost the game of airhockey, he went to Lyssa's side and took her hand.

They went over to the couch and sat down. Ryan turned on the TV and tuned to MTV-2. They slumped down into the cushions until their heads could not be seen by the others gathered around the airhockey table behind the couch. Their heads were touching, so they spoke softly.

"What'd you do today?" Ryan said.

"Picked a lot of blackberries."

"That pie was delicious."

"Well, it was made with the berries I picked, so I'm glad you liked it."

"Hey, I've got an idea. Let's go see Maddy."

Lyssa frowned. "What do you want do that for?"

"Because I want to see what she's like."

"I don't want to go see her."

"Then I'll go see her by myself."

"I don't know if Marie would like that."

"Marie doesn't have to know about it," Ryan said. "She and Hank are upstairs, probably watching *Law & Order* right now, or something. I just want to talk to her."

Still frowning, Lyssa shook her head. "She doesn't always talk. And sometimes when she does, she doesn't make any sense.

Sometimes it sounds like she's talking in a completely different language. I'm telling you, she's creepy."

"You want to know the real reason I want to see her?"

"What?"

He whispered in her ear, "I want to see her *because* she's creepy. I want to see what scared you so bad."

Lyssa sat up and looked back at the group around the airhockey table. They were absorbed in their game, cheering Nicole on, laughing. Lyssa slumped down again and said, "Okay. But we won't stay long. I don't want to get caught. I mean, Marie probably wouldn't mind *that* much, but she probably doesn't want us bothering Maddy, either."

They got up and left the rec room. They went down the hall and past the stairs, went on to the closed door of Maddy's room.

Lyssa knocked lightly with a knuckle and said, "Maddy? What're you doing?" She opened the door and stepped in.

Ryan followed her.

It was a large room with blue-sky wallpaper spotted with white fluffy clouds. There were posters on the walls of kittens and puppies and ducklings, with captions like "Hang in there!" and "Friends are forever." Stuffed toys were everywhere—on the bed, the dresser, on the floor here and there—and there were a lot of Barbie dolls. A dollhouse stood in the corner. There were Barbie accessories all over the room. A radio on the dresser played classical music softly.

Maddy sat in a chair against the wall. She sat with her back straight, hands in her lap. She wore a blue dress and white bunny-rabbit slippers on her feet. She appeared to be staring at the doorway when they entered, almost as if she'd been waiting for them. She was, indeed, a big girl for nine years old—fleshy and stout, with a large head and a small face. Her dark hair fell in curly strands to her shoulders.

Ryan and Lyssa stood just inside the door after Ryan closed it.

"Hi, Maddy," Lyssa said. "You listening to some music?"

After a moment, Maddy nodded her head once.

Lyssa took a step forward. "I brought someone to meet you, Maddy. His name is Ryan."

Ryan walked over to Maddy with his hand out to shake. "Hi, Maddy. Nice to meet you."

She stared at his hand a moment, then looked up at him, but she did not shake.

Ryan dropped his hand to his side, then hunkered down so his eyes were level with Maddy's. Her narrow brown eyes looked at him, but seemed to see through him, as if he weren't there. "I live here, too," he said. "I've been here three months. How long have you been here?"

Maddy blinked, and her eyes came into focus. She looked directly into Ryan's eyes and her lips parted. Her mouth turned up in a smile, creating dimples in her fat cheeks and revealing two rows of small white teeth.

"I've been here a long, long time," she said in a low, gravelly voice. It was the voice of someone who'd been smoking for years.

It startled Ryan. His mouth opened but he couldn't speak for a moment. The voice was startlingly incongruous—how had it come out of this little girl? Okay, she wasn't so little, but she wasn't the owner of that voice, she couldn't be. And yet it had come from her mouth.

"See what I mean?" Lyssa whispered behind him.

"How long have you been in the house?"

"Oh, in this house," Maddy said in the low, quiet voice. "You think small, boy. You'll never be a writer thinking that way."

"*What*?" Ryan said, his voice breathy with shock. Gooseflesh prickled across his back. The room suddenly felt chilly.

Maddy blinked and turned her gaze over Ryan's shoulder. "Hi, Lyssa," she said, and she sounded like a little girl, with a slightly adenoidal but distinctly girlish voice.

"Hi, Maddy. I brought Ryan to meet you."

Maddy looked at Ryan again. "Hi, Ryan."

"Hi," he said, his voice hoarse. He stood.

Maddy sniffed noisily. "Where's Marie?"

Lyssa said, "She's upstairs."

"Could I have a drink of water?"

"Sure, honey," Lyssa said. "Where's your glass?"

Maddy got up and waddled over to her bedstand and got her glass, waddled over to Lyssa and gave it to her. Lyssa took it to the bathroom across the hall and filled it, brought it back. Maddy took the glass in both hands and made slurping sounds as she drank from it, then took it over to the bedstand and set it down.

"Thank you," Maddy said.

"We should go," Lyssa said.

"Yeah, okay," Ryan said, going to the door.

"Nice to meetchew, Ryan," Maddy said.

He turned to her. Her face had a pinched quality to it, and she had about her the look and demeanor of someone who was, to be generous, slow. Ryan nodded and said, "Yeah, it was nice to meet you, too, Maddy." There was a slight tremble in his voice.

In the rec room, the airhockey game was still going on loudly. Ryan and Lyssa returned to the couch in front of the television.

Ryan said nothing for a long time. He was shaken by what Maddy had said to him in that strange gravelly voice. No one knew of Ryan's writing. Even though Ryan had asked him some questions about writing, even Mr. Granger did not know that Ryan wrote, only that he was interested in writing. His stories were hand-written in spiral-bound notebooks. He'd been writing them since he was ten years old. His journal was new—he'd never kept one until Mr. Granger had suggested it.

There was no way Maddy could know he wanted to be a writer. No one knew that but Ryan.

"What's the matter?" Lyssa said.

"Huh? What do you mean?"

"You look ... I don't know, like you saw a ghost, or something. Did she say something that bothered you?"

Ryan said nothing.

"See what I mean? There's something wrong with her."

"How did she talk like that?" Ryan whispered. "I mean, that voice. It was like a man's voice, a man who's been smoking two packs a day for years."

"Now you know what I was talking about. She said something that bothered you, didn't she? What was that about you being a writer?"

Ryan slouched a little lower on the couch and Lyssa came in close, their heads touching again.

"You can tell me," she whispered. "I won't tell anyone."

"I like to write," he said. "I write stories. I hope to be a writer. But nobody knows that. Nobody. You're the first person in the world I've ever told."

She smiled and took his hand. "Really? I'm the first?"

He nodded and returned her smile. "I've never told anyone because it's the kind of thing most people discourage. You know, they say, 'That's a hard business to get into,' or, 'You'll never make much money writing,' stuff like that. And I just never wanted to hear that, so I haven't told anyone. But it's what I've always wanted to do."

"Would you let me read your stories?" Lyssa said. "I'd really love to read them."

"Maybe."

"Have you ever let anyone read them?"

He shook his head. "Mr. Granger next door is a writer, though, and he said he'd like to read them, so I may type them up on the computer and print them and let him."

"But how did Maddy know you wanted to be a writer?"

"That's what I mean. There's no way she could know. It's impossible."

Lyssa's eyes widened and her brow furrowed. "Then ... what she said to me might be true."

"What?"

"She said sadness would follow me all my life." She looked about to cry. "If she knew about your writing—something she couldn't possibly know—then maybe she was right about that, too."

"Hey." Ryan put an arm around her and held her close. He didn't want her to cry. He couldn't stand it when anyone cried—it always made him want to cry, and he didn't want to do that in front of Lyssa. "Who knows what she was talking about. She's just a little retarded girl. Right?"

"But you just said—"

"I just said, she's just a little retarded girl. Right?"

Lyssa sniffled, and nodded against his shoulder. "You wanna get together later tonight?" she whispered.

Ryan thought about it a moment. He thought about that fat little girl sitting in her room listening to classical music. He wondered what her story was.

"Not tonight," he said.

"How come?"

"I want to do some writing tonight."

"Will you let me read it?"

He smiled. "Maybe."

But writing was not all he had in mind.

From the Journal of Ryan Kettering

I don't sleep much. I never have. I can get by on three or four hours of sleep in a night. I like to read and write at night while everyone else is sleeping. Along with writing, I read a lot. Reading is how I learned to write.

Even if I needed the sleep tonight, I don't think I could get it. I can't stop thinking about Maddy.

Instead of meeting with Lyssa tonight, I went to Maddy's room. I have a powerful little penlight I use for light when I move around the house at night, so I don't run into anything and make noise. I have to be careful when I get up and walk around in the middle of the night. It's a creaky old house, and Marie knows every single creak in the place. Once I get down the stairs without waking anyone, I'm home free.

I couldn't get over what Maddy had said to me, and it wasn't just that she knew about my wanting to be a writer. I had asked Maddy how long she'd been here, and in that deep voice, she'd said, "I've been here a long, long time." But when I asked the second time, I was more specific: "How long have you been in the house?" Then she'd said, "Oh, in this house. You think small, boy. You'll never be a writer thinking that way."

What had she meant by, "Oh, in this house?" What else did she think I meant when I asked her how long she'd been here? What did she mean when she said that I think small?

What the hell's wrong with her, anyway?

I had to talk to her some more, even if I had to wake her up.

The basement hall was dark, but there was light coming from under Maddy's door. Was she awake, or did she just leave a light on at night? I went to the door and considered knocking, but decided against it. I opened the door and went in.

The lamp on her nightstand was on and Maddy was sitting up on the edge of the bed, looking at me. I froze where I stood for a few seconds, I couldn't move. She looked like she'd been sitting

there waiting for me. She wore a pale green nightgown and her
hair was a mess. Strands of it dangled in her face. Her feet were
bare.

I looked around at all the toys. I couldn't understand where
she'd gotten so many expensive toys. A couple were still in their
boxes and hadn't even been opened yet. Hank and Marie are
always talking about how tight money is. If they're spending it on
Barbie accessories for Maddy, I'm not surprised.

"Hi, Maddy," I whispered as I closed the door. I didn't have to
whisper, there was no way anyone upstairs would hear me down in
the basement, but I whispered, anyway. "Remember me?"

"Ryan," she said, and she sounded like a sniffly, slow little girl.

"That's right," I said. There was a chair against the wall, the same
chair she'd been sitting in when I was down there earlier. I got it,
moved it over to the side of the bed, and sat down facing her. "How
are you tonight, Maddy?"

Instead of replying, she bowed her head. She looked like she was
praying. She stayed that way for about fifteen seconds and didn't
say anything.

"Maddy?" I said.

She lifted her head. Her small piggy eyes seemed narrower
now. "You've come back," Maddy said in that deep voice that
sounded damaged by cigarettes. "Curiosity killed the cat, you
know."

That voice gave me a chill. It didn't sound right. It sounded too
smart, too adult to be coming out of a young mentally-handicapped
girl like Maddy.

"Satisfaction brought him back," I said, but I don't think I
sounded too confident.

"What would satisfy you, Ryan?"

She kept smiling, with her head tilted forward just a little, those
strands of hair in her face, those dimples in her cheeks.

I asked the first question that came into my head, even though I
knew it didn't seem to make sense. But it felt right, because I didn't
feel like I was talking to Maddy anymore. I wasn't talking to that
fat little girl.

"Who are you?" I said.

"Thinking bigger, I see."

"What does that mean?" I said.

She shrugged. "It means you're thinking bigger, that's all. Opening your mind to ... possibilities."

"Who are you?"

"I'm just li'l ol' Maddy, Ryan. Who do you *think* I am?"

"Why does your voice sound like that?" I was still whispering.

Maddy chuckled. It sounded like a couple bricks being knocked together.

"Why did you come here tonight, Ryan?" the deep voice asked.

"How did you know about my writing?"

"I know lots of things." She said something in another language then. It sounded like French, but I wasn't sure.

"What?" I said.

"*Parlez-vous francais*, Ryan? I guess not." She stopped smiling.

"I don't speak French. What did you just say?"

"What does it matter? I'm just a little retarded girl, right? Right, Ryan? I'm just a little retarded girl."

I had the feeling I was being laughed at, toyed with, and it was irritating. But at the same time, it was scary, because I knew the girl sitting before me would not be capable of toying with someone, she wasn't sophisticated enough. Besides, how could she know what I'd said to Lyssa about her, that she was "just a little retarded girl"? And what was a mentally handicapped nine-year-old girl doing speaking French?

"What do you do all day?" I whispered.

"Oh, I do all kinds of things. You don't think I stay here all the time, do you? I have a very active life. But the things I like to do would not interest you. You would be ... quite horrified, I'm sure."

"Try me."

"Well, let's see. I helped a man beat a baby to death a little while ago. Just a little baby. But it wouldn't stop crying, and it got on the man's nerves. All it took was a little prompting from me, and he went for it."

"Went for ... what?"

She smiled again, even bigger this time. "The baby, of course. He beat it with his fists. He'd had a few drinks, which only loosened him up. He kept beating it till it stopped crying. But he caved its little skull in. Once he realized what he'd done, he didn't take it very well. His wife called the police, but before they could get there, the man put a loaded revolver in his mouth and blew the back of his head off, right in front of his wife and two little kids. It was a powerful family moment I'm sure they'll all remember for many, many years to come."

My mouth and throat were dry, and when I gulped, my throat made a little clicketing sound. I had to clear my throat before I could say anything.

"If you can leave," I said, "then why do you stay here?"

"Because I choose to. I have work to do here. *We* have work to do here."

"We? We who?"

"You're full of questions, aren't you, Ryan?" She said something in another language again, a different language than before.

"Was that ... German?" I said.

"You have a good ear. Now, why don't you go fuck your little girlfriend and leave me alone."

I was so surprised by these words coming out of Maddy that I flinched a little.

"How do you know about Lyssa and me?" I said.

"I know lots of things. I know that if you stay down here, you're going to get into trouble. I know that, in a little more than three minutes, Marie is going to wake up and put on her robe and walk through the house. Did you know she does that sometimes at night? And she's going to come down here and look in on me. And if she finds you here, you're going to be in trouble."

I knew that Marie sometimes got up in the middle of the night and wandered around the house, just checking things out. She'd found me in the kitchen a couple times, sitting at the table writing. She didn't mind that I was up, as long as I wasn't keeping others awake. But I knew she wouldn't approve of me being in Maddy's room in the middle of the night.

It wasn't until I was back up here in my bed that it occurred to me that I'd believed Maddy that Marie was going to wake up and come downstairs. I didn't even question it, I believed it right away and left her bedroom, came back upstairs.

Sure enough, as I was getting back in bed, I heard Marie get up and walk down the hall, down the stairs. How had Maddy known she was going to get up?

How could Maddy speak French so well? Or German? And how could she speak in that voice? It was a man's voice, or the voice of a woman who's been smoking unfiltered Camels for fifty years. It was very different than the other voice she used, the little-girl voice.

I'm not going to sleep very well tonight. I just know it.

FOUR

The next morning, Ryan mowed Mr. Granger's back lawn right after breakfast. He mowed the Prestons' lawn, too, with Hank's mower, then swept the grass off the front porch. He sat with Lyssa and talked for a little while. He took out the garbage for Marie, then asked if she and Hank could spare him for awhile. He did not have to work that day, and he wanted to spend some of it at Fortress of Solitude Comics in Anderson. Marie said he could go, so he got on his bike and rode down Fig Tree, turned left on Airport. He rode down the hill and across the Sacramento River, where Airport Road became North Street, which went through the center of Anderson. The Fortress was on North Street across from the police station, between a beauty parlor and a travel agency. Ryan leaned his bike against the wall just outside the comic book shop and went inside.

"Hey, Ryan," Max said.

Max was forty-five, a big guy. He was tall, but also quite wide. He always wore a baseball cap, and his greying black hair fell from beneath it to his shoulders. He never quite grew a beard, but he was always unshaved and stubbly.

"Hey, Max," Ryan said. "'Sup?"

"Same ol' same ol'."

The Fortress of Solitude was Max's shop. Ryan could not possibly afford to buy all the comic books he enjoyed reading, but Max didn't mind if he came to the shop and read them there. Max enjoyed having people around to talk comic books, and Ryan wasn't the only one who came into the shop just to hang around and talk and read comics.

Ryan found the new issue of *The Incredible Hulk* and took it to the front of the shop. He leaned a hip against the front counter as he opened the book and thumbed through it. Max sat on a chair behind the counter.

"Do you have a tape recorder I could borrow, Max?" Ryan said.

"No, afraid not. Why?"

"You speak any other languages?"

"Oh, a little French."

"How about German?"

"*Nein, mein fuhrer.* Why?"

"Do you know anybody who speaks German?"

"No. Why?"

"How well do you speak French?"

Max rolled one round shoulder. "I dunno. So-so, I guess. Why?"

"If I recorded someone saying something in French and played the recording for you, would you be able to tell me what that person was saying?"

"Probably. I could at least give you some idea what they're saying, if not a word-for-word translation. Why?"

Ryan started reading the comic book.

"Excuse me, but *why*?" Max said.

"Oh, it's nothing."

"Nothing? You gonna bring me a tape of somebody speaking French? Who do you know speaks French?"

Ryan didn't know what to tell him. He didn't think he should tell him the truth yet, if ever. How would he explain such a thing to Max? If Max heard that deep, gravelly voice, he'd never believe it was a nine-year-old girl speaking.

"It's kind of a long story, Max, I don't really want to get into it. I'll tell you when I bring in the tape, okay?" But he doubted he would play the tape for Max, if he ever recorded one. He needed someone who would be more open-minded.

"Eh, fine," Max said with a dismissive wave.

Byron and Richie came in, and before long, Ryan was involved with them and Max in a heated discussion about the Fantastic Four. After that subject faded, Richie brought up a new one.

Richie was seventeen, with a shaved head, a mangy blond goatee, and a few piercings in his right eyebrow. He was a talker, fond of the sound of his own voice. His father was a cop who worked nights out of the station across the street.

"Did you hear about the guy who beat his baby to death last night?" Richie said.

Ryan sat in a chair behind the counter with Max, reading an old *Silver Surfer*, and he dropped the comic book into his lap when Richie spoke. "*What?*" he said as he stood. He snatched up the comic book before it could fall from his thighs to the floor. "What did you say, Richie?"

"Some guy here in Anderson last night," Richie said, "beat his little baby to death. With his fists. Because the baby wouldn't stop crying. My dad took the call."

Ryan dropped back down into the chair. He felt like he'd been punched in the gut.

"Beat the baby's skull right in," Richie said.

Ryan licked his lips. "Don't tell me the guy ate his gun, too," he said.

"Yeah, how'd you know?" Richie said. "Did you hear about it already?"

"What's the matter with you, Ryan?" Byron said. He was a plump guy of medium height with sandy hair that always looked like it needed to be trimmed. He wore an Electra T-shirt and jeans. Byron was a big Daredevil fan. "You know the guy, or something?"

"No," Ryan said, shaking his head.

"Well, you look upset."

"Oh. No. I mean, just that ... well, that's pretty low, right? Beating up a baby?"

"Oh, yeah, sure it is," Byron said with a shrug.

Richie changed the subject again, but Ryan was no longer paying attention. He was thinking about Maddy, and that deep, gruff voice.

Elliott Granger wanted to ignore the doorbell. He was immersed in his book, deeply involved, and it was coming along so smoothly. The doorbell couldn't ring at a worse time. He typed to the end of the paragraph he was writing, then turned his chair toward his walker.

"Dammit," he muttered as he stood and clutched the walker on each side. He leaned on it as he pushed it ahead of him out of the office and down the hall. The front door was open. His cats, Mona and Lisa, liked to sit there and look out the security door—it was like television for them—so sometimes he locked the security door and left the front door open. Sure enough, the cats were there on their haunches, staring up at Ryan, who stood just outside the door. As soon as Elliott saw the boy, he tried to get the scowl off his face.

"I hope I'm not bothering you," Ryan said.

"Not at all, Ryan." He shooed the cats away and unlocked the door. Ryan opened it and came inside, pulled it closed behind him. "What can I do for you?"

"I was wondering, um, do you have a tape recorder I could borrow?" Ryan said.

"A tape recorder? Well, I've got a few. What kind do you need?"

Ryan shrugged. "What kind do you have?"

"Let's go take a look."

Elliott led Ryan down the hall to his office. He sat in his chair at his large L-shaped desk. He opened the bottom drawer and removed two tape recorders. One used standard cassette tapes and wasn't much larger than one, while the other was a small microcassette recorder.

"Wow," Ryan said, "this one's small." He picked up the microcassette recorder. "Could I borrow this one?"

"Sure. You can use the tape that's in it. I've got more tapes, if you need them."

"Just the one will be fine," Ryan said. "I promise I'll take good care of it."

"I know you will, Ryan. What are you using it for?"

"Well ... " Ryan looked down at his feet for a moment. Then he looked at Elliott again and said, "Do you speak French?"

"No, I'm afraid not."

"How about German?"

"No, not that, either. I have enough trouble with English. But I know people who are bi- and multilingual. Why?"

Ryan chewed on his lower lip a moment. "I'm going to record someone speaking another language with this recorder. If I bring it back to you, do you think you could figure out what that person's saying?"

"Well, if I couldn't, I probably know someone I can call who could. Who is this person?"

He chewed on his lower lip again for a moment. "Would you mind if I told you later, when I bring the tape back? It might be easier then."

Elliott nodded. "Sure. Okay." He smiled. "I'm intrigued. Does this have something to do with a story you're working on, by any chance?"

Ryan frowned. "No, it doesn't. I really wish it did, it would be so much easier then. But, no, it doesn't. Thank you for the recorder. I'll bring it back in a day or two."

"Sure. No rush."

Elliott followed him out, said goodbye at the door. He frowned as he made his way back to his office. The boy had looked so troubled when he'd answered Elliott's question. He'd looked almost afraid.

"You've been busy," Maddy said in that deep, gravelly voice. She spoke just above a whisper. She sat on the edge of her bed as she had the night before.

It was just past one o'clock in the morning. Ryan had taken the chair from the wall again and this time sat on it backwards. He folded his arms across the top of the chair's back and rested his chin on his arm.

"What do you mean?" Ryan said.

"You know what I mean. Don't waste my time by playing dumb."

"I haven't been any busier than usual."

"Don't bullshit a bullshitter." She cleared her throat. "Am I talking loudly enough for your recorder to pick me up clearly?"

Ryan silently cursed. He had the microcassette recorder in his shirt pocket. It was recording. How did she know?

"I'm not a show-and-tell item, kid," she said. "Don't fuck with me."

Thumbs pressed hard over Ryan's throat. He could not breathe. He sat up straight with a jerk, grabbed at his throat with his hands, but there was nothing there. And yet hands squeezed his throat. He stood up, and still clawed at his neck for a few seconds even after he'd started taking gasping breaths. There was no longer any pressure on his throat, nor did he have the sensation that any had been applied recently. Chest heaving, he put the chair back in its place against the wall, then headed for the door.

"Don't leave, Ryan," Maddy said in her normal little-girl voice. "Please stay."

Ryan stopped and turned back. Maddy sat up straight on the bed, head cocked to one side, a sad frown on her forehead.

"Maddy?"

She lifted her head and smiled. The deep voice said, "She really likes you, Ryan."

Ryan took a step back, reached up and touched his throat. "Are you going to do that again?" he said.

"Just making a point," the voice said as Maddy relaxed her posture a little. Her shoulders and back slumped slightly.

"Making a threat, you mean."

"No, I don't make threats, really," it said, very politely. "If that's how you took it, I apologize, it wasn't a threat, really. I was just making a point."

He rubbed his throat with his right hand. "I don't know if I want to talk to you anymore."

"But I haven't done any tricks for your recorder yet. Taw druck coe-nawsk agwinn. Glay urrum niece day-knee."

"*What?*"

A bit louder and more clearly enunciated: "Taw druck coe-nawsk agwinn. Glay urrum niece day-knee. Idiots."

Ryan hoped the recorder had gotten all that, because he hadn't understood a word of it. It didn't sound like any language he'd heard before.

Maddy looked directly into his eyes again and smirked as she said, "*Votre pere etait l'un de trafiquants de la drogue de votre mere. Il l'a baisee dans une ruelle. Vous avez ete concu pres d'une pile des ordures.*"

The door opened and Ryan gasped as he spun around. He expected to see Marie standing in the doorway, but it was Lyssa. She frowned at him as she stepped inside and closed the door.

"What the hell are you doing in *here?*" she said.

Maddy grinned and said in her normal voice, "Hello, Lyssa."

"Hi, Maddy," Lyssa said. "How ya doin', hon?"

"I'm fine."

"What have you and Ryan been talking about?"

"I don't know."

"You don't know?"

Ryan reached into his pocket and turned off the tape recorder. "C'mon, Lyssa," he said as he took her elbow. "Let's go."

There were questions Ryan wanted to ask Maddy, but the strangling incident had shaken him badly. Somehow, he would be much more comfortable talking with Maddy when there was sunlight pouring in through the three narrow windows high on the wall beside her bed. He took Lyssa's elbow and led her out of the bedroom.

"I'll see you later, Maddy," Lyssa said over her shoulder, but the child said nothing in response.

Ryan pulled the door closed and used his penlight to get them down the dark hall and into the rec room. There, he turned on the long fluorescent light trays overhead. They sat on the couch and he turned on the TV with the volume low, tuned to the Cartoon Network.

"What's the matter?" Lyssa said. "Something's wrong."

"What do you know about Maddy?"

"Nothing, really."

"Hasn't Marie said *anything* about her? Where she came from? What happened to her parents?"

"No, she hasn't said a word. I've only helped her dress Maddy a couple times."

"What about the others—Candy and Nicole, Gary and Keith. Have they ever said anything about her?"

"The others don't talk about Maddy."

"She speaks French. And German. And some other language I don't even recognize."

"That's impossible. She's only nine. Maybe it only *sounded* like French and German."

Ryan took the tape recorder from his pocket, rewound it, played it for a few seconds, then fast forwarded it. He found the spot where Maddy spoke in French and played it for Lyssa. He said, "Does that sound like it just *sounds* like French to you?"

"I'm telling you, Ryan, there's something wrong with that girl.

And I'm not talking about her handicap. I mean, there's something ... something ... *sinister* about her."

He nodded. "Yes, there is. I'd like to find out what it is."

They decided to go to bed before Marie went on one of her patrols and found them in the rec room watching television. The rules were that the television went off at ten o'clock, and stayed off for the night. They kissed at the foot of the basement stairs, then went up to their rooms.

Ryan lay in his bed staring into the dark for two hours before sleep finally came.

Maddy scared him.

FIVE

Elliott was eating a bowl of Grape Nuts at his desk and reading the headlines when the doorbell rang. He hoped it was Ryan with the tape recorder—he was very interested in hearing the boy's story.

Sure enough, Ryan stood at the door. Elliott let him in and led him down the hall to the office. "Have a seat," Elliott said, waving toward the only chair in the office other than his own. It was stacked with magazines. "Just put those on the floor."

Ryan removed the magazines and moved the chair closer to Elliott's desk. He held the microcassette recorder in his right hand.

"Do you mind if I play something for you?" Ryan said.

"Please do."

Ryan pushed the button and set the recorder on the desk.

A deep male voice said, "Taw druck coe-nawsk agwinn. Glay urrum niece day-knee."

Something about the deep, whisky-voice made Elliott frown. He wasn't sure why yet, but he didn't like the voice. It made him feel ... uncomfortable.

Ryan's voice said, "*What?*"

Then, louder and clearer: "Taw druck coe-nawsk agwinn. Glay urrum niece day-knee. Idiots" Shortly after that, the same voice said, "*Votre pere etait l'un de trafiquants de la drogue de votre mere. Il l'a baisee dans une ruelle. Vous avez ete concu pres d'une pile des ordures.*"

Ryan turned off the recorder with a click. "What did that sound like to you?"

Elliott felt tightness in his neck. The voice had made him tense up. It was an unsettling voice. The word "corrupt" came to Elliott's mind.

"Well, those last lines were definitely spoken in French," Elliott said. "Something about your mother and father."

"What? Really?"

"That's all I could make out, though. Like I said, I don't speak French."

"What about the other?"

"That sounded like Gaelic to me. I don't know for sure, but I know someone who would." Elliott took the cordless phone from its base on the desk. As he punched in a number, he said, "I know a writer in Los Angeles named Francis Feighan. He knows Gaelic, and I think he might know some French, too. In fact, Francis knows a little bit of everything." He put the phone to his ear. Along with the purring sound of the phone at the other end ringing, he heard a crackle of static. He hit the Channel button on the phone a few times, but it didn't help.

"Who's this?" Francis said, as he always did when he answered the phone.

"It's Elliott, Francis."

They exchanged pleasantries and a little small talk.

"What's with the connection?" Francis said.

"I don't know," Elliott said. "You hear that static, too?"

"Yeah."

"I'm going to hang up and call you again," Elliott said. He severed the connection, punched the Redial button, and put the phone to his ear. The static had not gone away.

"It's still there," Francis said.

"Oh, well," Elliott said. "Look, Francis, I want to play something for you."

Ryan rewound the tape a bit and handed the recorder to Elliott, who put it up to the phone's mouthpiece. He hit the Play button. First, the Gaelic-sounding lines, then the French.

"Did you hear that, Francis?" Elliott said.

Francis said, "I couldn't make out the first part, but I heard the French."

"Can you translate?"

"Yeah." Francis translated the lines.

Elliott frowned and looked at Ryan.

"Repeat that," Elliott said. As Francis repeated it, Ryan wrote it down on a Post-It pad.

"Play that first part again," Francis said. "It was Gaelic, but I couldn't make it out through this damned static."

Elliott rewound the tape a bit, then hit Play again. After the lines were spoken twice, he hit Stop.

Francis laughed through the static. "Is this some kind of joke?" he said.

"What do you mean?" Elliott said.

"It's Gaelic, all right. It's Gaelic for, 'We have a bad connection. Call me later.' And then, 'Idiots,' but that was in English. What is this you're playing for me?"

It was a hot summer morning and Elliott had not turned on the air conditioner yet, but he felt a chill fall over him as if he were sitting in a cold draft. He looked at Ryan again. "I'm not sure. Let me get back to you. Thanks, Francis." He put the phone back on its base and turned to Ryan. "Okay. What's the story, Ryan?"

"What does that stuff mean?" Ryan asked.

"First, if you don't mind, I'd appreciate it if you told me who's on this tape and why he's speaking in Gaelic and French."

"Well ... " Ryan looked at his lap for a moment, then around at the office. "I'm afraid you won't believe me."

"Why wouldn't I believe you?"

"Because that voice on the tape isn't a he. It's a nine-year-old girl."

Frowning, Elliott picked up the small recorder and rewound for a few seconds, then hit Play again. He listened to the deep, gravelly voice. It got under his skin and made him nervous. There was something ... *bad* ... about the voice—he could think of no better way to describe it. He put down the recorder, picked up the bowl of cereal, leaned back in his chair and said, "Okay. My mind is open. Let's hear it."

Elliott ate his Grape Nuts and listened as Ryan told him about Maddy. He told him about the things Maddy had said to him in that deep voice, the thing she knew about him that no one could possibly know, and about the man who'd beaten his baby to death then blown his brains out.

"You're serious?" Elliott said when Ryan was finished. "I mean, about that being a little *girl* on that tape?"

"Well, she's not so little," Ryan said, "but yeah." He rewound the tape all the way and played the whole thing for him.

Elliott heard Maddy's slightly adenoidal little-girl voice as well as the deep, rich, smoky voice that spoke so knowingly to Ryan.

More than once, Elliott found himself gulping air. He felt a tightness in his chest. He wanted to listen to the tape again, but he had the feeling Ryan wanted to talk. The boy's eyebrows were huddled above his nose and he kept chewing on his lower lip. He looked anxious, troubled.

Elliott took in a deep breath and let it out slowly. He said, "I don't suppose there's any chance Maddy has a police scanner in her bedroom?"

"I didn't see one," Ryan said. "Why?"

Elliott shrugged. "Well, it would explain her knowledge of the baby beating and suicide."

"True. But I didn't see one, really. Just a radio and lots of Barbie toys."

"There's a silent patch on the tape, and then you talk about the gir—uh, about the voice making a threat. What happened there?"

Ryan hesitated. "Something ... something closed my throat. It was like there were hands on my throat, and I couldn't breathe. But there was nothing there. Then it stopped, just as suddenly as it had started." Ryan sat forward on the front edge of the chair. "Did your friend translate what she said in French, Mr. Granger?"

"Yes, he did." Elliott looked at the translation of the French lines written on the Post-It pad. Something made him not want to read them to the boy. A dull, distant alarm went off in his mind—he knew the words he'd written down would hurt Ryan. But he could hardly refuse to share them. "Well, the Gaelic translation—it turns out that it *is* Gaelic—was very strange. We had a bad connection on the phone, there was a lot of static, and I had to replay the Gaelic lines for Francis because he didn't get them the first time through the static, and it turns out the ... the voice is saying, 'We have a bad connection. Call me later.' And then it refers to someone as 'Idiots.'" Elliott felt another brief chill. "Now I know how strange this sounds, but I've got this feeling in my gut that that little jibe, that 'Idiots' at the end, there, was meant *specifically* for Francis and myself. Isn't that crazy?"

"That's what I mean, Mr. Granger. That girl, Maddy, she's got me thinking all kinds of crazy things. She—" Ryan leaned farther forward and lowered his voice near a whisper, as if he were telling

Elliott a secret he wanted no one else to hear. "She *knew* you were going to have a bad connection."

"Maybe ... maybe she's somehow responsible for the connection being bad," Elliott said, quietly, thinking out loud. His eyes met Ryan's and he realized the boy thought that wasn't such a crazy idea.

Ryan sat with his hands on his spread knees, body tilted forward, eyebrows suddenly high. "I wouldn't be surprised. It says it doesn't stay there in the basement all the time."

"Wait a second, wait a second," Elliot said. He put the empty bowl on his desk, leaned back in his chair, and locked his hands behind his head, elbows out. "What are we saying, here? There's probably a perfectly good explanation for her behavior. She's mentally handicapped, right? Maybe she has a personality disorder, maybe a *multiple* personality disorder. Maybe that's why she's kept to herself. We could be reading things into this and getting ourselves all worked up over—"

"Did I read something into that guy who beat his baby to death then shot himself?" Ryan said.

Frowning, Elliott slowly lowered his arms to the chair's armrests. "No. No, you didn't."

"Mr. Granger, what was the translation of the other lines? She said something in French."

"Yeah, that." He picked up the Post-It pad. "She said, 'Your father was one of your mother's drug dealers. He screwed her in an alley. You were conceived on a pile of garbage.'"

Ryan's eyebrows remained high for a long time. Moving as slowly as molasses, he sunk back in the chair and slumped there. Tears spread over the bottom edges of his eyes and sparkled there for awhile. One finally spilled over the edge and crept down his cheek.

"I'm sorry, Ryan, I didn't mean to upset you," Elliott said.

"S'okay. It's just that ... I believe her. She knows. *It* knows. How does it know?"

Elliott played the entire tape again and listened carefully, his eyes narrowed and intense. Both voices came from the same nine-year-old child. Even if she had multiple personalities, she would be limited by her knowledge, her lack of maturity. It was as if an adult were speaking through the child.

And that's crazy talk, Elliott thought, *especially coming from someone like you. Possession is horror talk, not real-life talk.*

But what other explanation was there?

"Maybe I should talk to Marie about her," Elliott said.

"What do you mean?"

"I might be able to find out something about Maddy, where she came from, what her situation is."

"Would you tell me?"

"Sure. I'll give Marie a call today, come up with some excuse for her to come over."

"Thanks, Mr. Granger."

"So, you've already written some stories, huh?"

"Yeah. They're all written in notebooks. I could type them up and print them out if you'd really like to read them."

"I would. Do that."

"Okay."

Elliott walked Ryan to the front door. Out on the porch, Ryan looked over at the Preston house.

"Who's that, I wonder?" Ryan said.

Elliott leaned out the door and looked over at the big house next door. Two dark Lexus sedans were parked in front. It looked like they had government plates, but he wasn't positive at that distance. It was common to see government cars in front of the Preston house, usually driven by social workers—but not usually such *nice* government cars. Apparently, they had just pulled up, because the doors opened and people were getting out. Men in dark suits and sunglasses.

"I'm going to go see what's up," Ryan said.

Elliott said goodbye and Ryan headed off for the house. Elliott remained in the doorway for awhile, watching the men. A woman was the last to get out. She was silver-haired and wore a smart blue suit. She was the only one not wearing shades, but she wore glasses. A tall, balding man with grey hair sidled up to her and they stopped and spoke a moment. They were joined by a short greying man with dark hair and a mustache. The two men carried briefcases, and the woman had the strap of a satchel over her shoulder. There

were four other men and they all stood and looked around. They
looked to Elliott like security men who were quickly assessing the
area while the woman and two men talked.

He came inside and pulled the security door closed, locked it.
One of the cats meowed.

His chest felt tight and his stomach felt cramped from tension.
He was not sure why.

From the Journal of Ryan Kettering

There's some weird shit going down around here and it's starting to make me very nervous. Whatever's going on, I get the feeling it's been going on for awhile.

As I left Mr. Granger's house this morning, two black Lexus sedans pulled up to the house and a bunch of people got out. The cars had federal plates. These were government people. I could tell right away that four of them were agents of some kind—they were the guys who'd gotten out of the front seats of both cars. They all looked alike. I remembered seeing, in Toys-R-Us once, a Ken and Barbie set in which Ken and Barbie were dressed up like Mulder and Scully from *The X-Files*. These four guys looked like Ken-doll Mulder. Then there were three older people. A tall old guy who was bald on top, a shorter guy with a mustache, and a woman with white hair and glasses. The three of them stuck together and talked as they went up the front walk. The four suits followed. They were on the porch by the time I got to them, and the tall bald man had pressed the doorbell.

"Can I help you?" I said.

The four suits turned to me and looked me over.

"Hello, Ryan," one of them said.

That *really* gave me the creeps.

"We're here to see Marie and Hank," another one said.

They continued to look at me as the older people stepped back out of my way and let me in. When I opened the front door, Marie was just inside, on her way to answer the bell. She smiled at me, then saw the people behind me. For the first time since I'd moved in, I saw Marie's smile completely disappear. Her whole face went loose for a couple seconds and the color left her cheeks—her cheeks are always rosy—and her eyes got a little bigger. Then she cleared her throat and her face was back to normal—smiling and pleasant, but still not quite as rosy as before.

Marie went to the door and said, "Come in, come in. Just a

second." She turned to me, put her arm around me and slowly led me away from them, into the living room. "I want you to get the boys and I want you to go out back and water Hank's garden, then talk to Hank and see what he wants you to do next. All right? Will you do that for me, Ryan?"

I knew she wanted us out of the way. She'd probably give the girls something to keep them busy, too. She wanted our attention on other things.

"Who are those people?" I said. "And how do they know who *I* am?"

Still smiling, she said, "Never you mind who those people are, just do as I say, all right?"

"All right." I didn't like it, but there was nothing I could do about it. I headed upstairs to find Gary and Keith, then remembered Gary was at work. As I was going down the upstairs hall, I ran into Lyssa coming down the attic stairs. "Hey," I whispered as I went to her. I stood close. "There are some people downstairs. I have to go outside and water the garden, but do me a favor, okay?"

She nodded anxiously, her eyes wide.

"Try to keep track of what they do and say while they're here."

"What if I can't?"

"Do your best. I've got a feeling Marie's going to give you chores, but try to keep an eye on these people. I want to know why they're here."

"I'll do my best." She surprised me with a kiss, then smiled. It made me smile, too.

I got Keith—he was lying on his bottom bunk, beneath Gary's bed, reading a Spider-Man comic book—and we went out to the backyard. When we passed through the living room, Marie and the federal people were gone.

After watering the garden, Hank had us pick plums off the plum trees before the birds got them all. We put the plums in buckets, then emptied the buckets into cardboard boxes. On Saturday, we would take the boxes down to the end of the road in Hank's pick-up and set up a table at the Fig Tree Lane Flea Market, and we'd put the plums in Ziplock bags and sell them all by noon or one o'clock.

When it came time for me to leave for work, the two Lexuses

were still parked outside, but there was no sign of the five men and one woman inside. There was no sign of Lyssa, either. I hoped she was keeping her eyes open.

When I got back home from work, the sedans were gone, but there was a truck parked in front of the house, and men were moving things into the house on dollies. Ramps had been set up over the front steps.

I went inside to find Marie hovering over it all.

"What's going on?" I said.

"Oh, just some new things for the rec room," she said. "I think you boys will be very pleased."

Gary thundered up the basement stairs and punched me in the shoulder. "You see the stuff we're gettin'?" he said.

"No. What are we getting?"

"A big high-definition plasma TV with surround sound, a new DVD player and a buncha new DVDs, and four new arcade video games. Can you believe it?"

I looked at Marie, and I caught her eye, but only for a second. She looked away and didn't look at me again. It wasn't that she *didn't* look at me, she *wouldn't* look at me.

I found Lyssa in the dining room, setting the table for dinner.

"What's been going on here?" I whispered.

"I'll tell you later. After dinner in the rec room."

Over dinner, everyone was excited about the new stuff in the rec room and it was the main topic of conversation. Nobody asked where it had come from, or how Hank and Marie were able to afford it. Nobody but me, and I kept my thoughts to myself.

After dinner, everyone was in the rec room, playing the new games. Hank watched the news on the enormous new plasma flatscreen on the wall between the cupboards.

Lyssa and I went to the loveseat against the wall by the entrance to the hallway. With everyone talking and the television playing so loudly, we could talk about whatever we wanted unnoticed by the others.

"They were down here in Maddy's room," Lyssa said.

"All of them?" I said.

She nodded. "All seven of them. They were down here the whole time."

"Did you see or hear any of it?"

"No. Marie kept us busy upstairs. But I did hear *something*. Afterward, they came up to the dining room and met with Hank and Marie. I was in the kitchen cleaning up after lunch. Marie fed them, believe it or not."

"Of course she did," I said. "Marie feeds everybody."

Lyssa told me she'd overheard most of the meeting between Hank and Marie and the federal suits. The woman, Dr. Sempris, had done most of the talking, she said. She'd repeatedly reminded Hank and Marie "how very important it is that Maddy not interact with any of the other children living in the house. Of course, it's important she interact with no one but you, Mrs. Preston, but we're especially anxious to know that every precaution has been taken to prevent any interaction between Maddy and the other children in this home."

I was impressed by how well Lyssa remembered what was said. She said Marie had assured them that the other children in the house had no interest in Maddy and virtually ignored her.

"They seemed pretty happy about that," Lyssa said. "Then the woman, this Dr. Sempris, said, 'Now, Mr. And Mrs. Preston, what can we do to make this house a better place for these kids?' And Hank went down the list—a big high-definition plasma flatscreen with surround sound, a new DVD player, every Disney movie ever made on DVD, and some new arcade video games. And the woman said, 'I don't see a problem with that at all, do you?' and she turned to the bald man and he shook his head and said, 'No problem at all,' and the guy with the mustache said, 'I don't see a problem.' Then the woman said, 'They'll be delivered by this evening.' And then they left."

"Have you seen Maddy since then?" I asked.

"No."

"You haven't mentioned to anyone that I've gone down there to talk to her, have you?"

"Of course not."

"Good. Don't."

I played one of the new video games for awhile. As soon as I had the opportunity, I talked to Gary.

"Hey, you noticed those guys in suits who came here today?" I said.

Smiling, Gary nodded and said, "Yeah."

"Have they been here before?"

"Oh, yeah. I seen 'em a couple, three times. I think they come to see Maddy."

"Who are they?"

Gary shrugged. "I dunno. I figured maybe they was relatives, or somethin'. Wanna play another game?"

"Not right now."

Gary started playing one of the video games. I sneaked out and went next door to see Mr. Granger....

SIX

Elliott sat in his recliner looking at Ryan on the couch, and found himself trembling with fear and thinking, *What am I living next door to, anyway?* He was giving serious thought to the kinds of things he normally reserved for his fiction—like possession, either by some spirit or a demon—things he never thought he would be looking at realistically.

"What do you think it means, Mr. Granger?" Ryan said after a long silence.

Elliott thought, *I think it means either I'm having some kind of breakdown, or the fat little girl in the basement next door is possessed by something bad—something that people in the government apparently talk to every now and then.*

Ryan had told Elliott everything that had happened at the house that day—everything he knew about, at least—and about the new goodies that had been delivered shortly after the government people had gone.

"You're sure they were federal plates?" Elliott said.

Ryan nodded.

"How do you know?"

"Because I know city, county, and state plates, and they weren't any of those, but they were government plates."

Elliott nodded once—it made sense. Besides, he'd seen what Ryan had called the four Ken-doll Mulders, and they certainly looked the part.

"It means that the government is interested in Maddy, Ryan. That's the only explanation I can come up with. Why they would be interested in her, I don't know."

"Yeah, you do," Ryan said. He met Elliott's gaze levelly and didn't look away.

Elliott said nothing, but he knew the boy was right.

Ryan said, "They're interested in whatever it is that talks

through Maddy. It knows things. It can do things. And they've got her tucked away in this group home in this nowhere town where nobody'll know about her, hidden away in a place they can come to and talk to it when they need to."

Elliott saw that Ryan was trembling, too.

"Mr. Granger, I don't like the idea of living under the same roof as that thing."

"How would you feel about talking to it again?"

Ryan frowned. "Do you think I should?"

"Take the recorder again. Ask it what the government wants with it. See what it has to say. It probably won't tell you anything, but whatever it says, get it on tape. Then, tomorrow, I'm going to talk to Marie. I didn't call her today because I knew there were people over there and I figured she'd be busy. Then I saw that truck unloading things, and I figured she had plenty to deal with and left her alone. But I'll call her over tomorrow, and I'll play the tape for her."

"Wait, if she finds out I've been talking to Maddy—"

"I don't think you'll be in any trouble, Ryan. In fact, it might be a good idea to have you here when I tell her. We could tell her together. Maybe she doesn't know what she's keeping in the basement."

"How could she not know?"

"Maybe it doesn't show itself around her," Elliott said with a shrug. "This thing isn't always obvious, right?"

Still frowning, Ryan nodded. "That's true."

"Are the Prestons religious?"

"Marie goes to church every Sunday, but she's not, like, pushy about it, or anything. You're thinking Maddy's possessed, aren't you?"

"Well, I'd rather you didn't quote me on it, but given everything you've told me and what I've heard ... yes, it's crossed my mind."

"Whatever that thing is, it's bad. I mean, it's really bad. Just hearing that voice makes me feel ... I don't know, *dirty*. And it said it helped that man beat that baby to death. It *helped*."

"You said you asked why it stays in that house," Elliott said. "Tell me again what it said."

"Because it had a job to do. It said, '*We* have a job to do.'"

Elliott wished he could get up and pace, but with the walker and the painful hip, it just wasn't the same. Instead, he rubbed his jaw with his right hand, back and forth several times. Then he cracked his knuckles one at a time. He thought of the voice on the tape—the voice that made him deeply uncomfortable, that made him want to turn off the recorder because he didn't want to hear it anymore. He imagined that voice talking to those two briefcase-carrying men and their female companion. They looked important. Who were they? For what government agency did they work? What kind of questions would they ask the ... thing? What kind of *job* did it have to do?

"What the hell is it?" Elliott muttered as he rubbed his jaw again. He looked at Ryan again. "I'm sure Marie won't be too upset with you about talking to Maddy. You'll have me on your side. I think we need more on tape, though, more for her to listen to. Talk to Maddy one more time tonight, then you and I will talk to Marie tomorrow."

Ryan took in a deep breath as he nodded, let the breath out slowly with his cheeks puffed up. "Okay. I'll do it. I won't like it, but I'll do it."

From the Journal of Ryan Kettering

I just got back from Maddy's room and my hands are shaking so bad, I can't write very well. I may not be able to read this later. I had to go to the bathroom before I came back here to the bedroom. I nearly wet myself down there in the basement.

She laughed in that deep, husky voice as soon as I came into the room. I decided to stand and didn't bother with the chair this time. I noticed there were more Barbie accessories in the room, all unopened in their boxes.

"I bet you're just *full* of questions, aren't you, Ryan?" the voice said. "Well, ask away. 'Ask, and it shall be given you; seek, and ye shall find; knock, and it shall be opened unto you.'"

I got just enough religion to recognize those as the words of Jesus Christ, and even though I'm not religious at all, I was offended to hear them spoken by that rough, smoky voice, by that thing. My mouth was dry, and I had to work up some spit to talk. I nodded and said, "Yeah, that's from, what ... Matthew, right?"

"Ah, you remember your Sunday school lessons."

"They were beaten into me by a religious fanatic. He was somebody you'd probably really like."

"Not familiar with his work, I'm sorry, although I've done some work in that field myself. Child abuse. It's such fruitful work. I derive a great deal of pleasure from the effects as they become evident years later. There's no *end* to the neuroses that can, and do, come of it. It's a field in which I try to exercise as much creativity as possible. But I digress. What have you come to ask me, Ryan?"

"Those people," I said, my voice hoarse, "what do they want with you?"

"If I told you that, Ryan, I would have to kill you." It chuckled, that hard, dry sound, and a shudder went through me. After that, my bladder felt full. "Seriously, Ryan, I can't tell you that. It's privileged information. Top secret. That's why you're not even supposed to be talking to me right now. I'm a big secret, Ryan. We can't have wild young wards of the state running around knowing about a big secret like li'l ol' me, now, can we?"

"What do you tell them?"

"Oh, Ryan. You force me to say this—it's none of your damned business. But if you'd exercise your imagination, you might think of a few possibilities on your own, Ryan. Think about it. I *know* things. You know that. Your father, by the way, died two weeks after your fifth birthday. He was stabbed to death in a fight."

"How ... how do I know that's true?"

Maddy smiled. "You know it's true, Ryan. You know in your heart it's true, just as you knew it was the truth when Mr. Granger's friend translated what I said in French. It simply rang true, didn't it? Just as this rings true. He was stabbed to death in a fight when you were five. He never even knew about you."

"Who are you that you can know that?"

"Like I said ... I know things."

"That's not an answer. Who are you? *What* are you? Are you a demon?"

"Now you're getting personal, Ryan, and I find it very rude."

"*Are* you a demon? Or are you something else?"

"If I told you who and what I am and revealed my part in the great scheme of things, Ryan, your poor little head would explode. Let's leave it at that, okay?"

I shook my head. "That's still no answer."

In a perfect impersonation of Jack Nicholson, the voice said, "You can't *handle* the truth," but without speaking loudly. Then Maddy laughed a high Maddy laugh, with her real voice, moist and adenoidal, and said, "You're silly," before laughing some more. Then she became serious and her mouth curled up into an O for a moment before she said, "Help me, Ryan. Please help me." For that moment, her eyes became less focused and she swayed a little where she sat, on the edge of the bed. But focus returned and she smiled a very unpleasant smile. Then the voice said, "Next question."

I was pretty knocked over by what Maddy had said. The *real* Maddy, not that twisted voice. The little girl Maddy who'd said, "Help me, Ryan. Please help me." She'd sounded so sad and helpless and somehow urgent at the same time, it made me a little sick to my stomach.

"What's your job here?" I asked.

"My, but you're tenacious tonight. Why don't you ask me something I *can* answer. Like 'When is the world going to end?' or 'When will I die?' Something like that, okay?"

"What does the government want from you?" I asked.

Maddy rolled her eyes. "What do you *think* they want, you silly boy? Knowledge, they want *knowledge*. Knowledge I can give them."

"What do you get out of it?" I asked.

"I should make you wash out your mouth with your own urine. That would teach you to pry. I could, you know. Your bladder's pretty full about now, isn't it, Ryan? You gonna wet your pants?"

"What do you get out of it?" I asked again.

"There's a war going on. I provide them with information. They provide me with the only thing I'm interested in. Sacrifice."

"What kind of sacrifice?"

"What do you think?"

"Hu ... human sacrifice?"

A big smile fattened Maddy's cheeks and made her eyes small. "Every bomb dropped is a sacrifice to me. And the thing with me is, I don't care who's droppin' 'em or who they're bein' dropped on." It laughed that cold, hard laugh. "As long as the bombs keep droppin', the missiles keep flyin', I'm happy."

I didn't say anything for awhile. I thought of the bombs being dropped in the Middle East, of all the people being killed on all sides. She kept smiling that big smile at me.

"And now that I've told you," it said, "I'll have to kill you."

"How old are you?" I said quickly, wanting to change the subject.

"Older than you could possibly imagine living."

"Are you ... evil?"

"That's a matter of opinion, Ryan, and don't believe anyone who tells you otherwise. Yes, I helped the man beat his baby to death. But I also spared that child a nightmarish childhood at the hands of her abusive father, and I rid the world of a child abuser. Everything has its positive side, Ryan."

That's evil, I thought, but I didn't say it, I know I didn't say it.

"Too bad, Ryan. I expected something more original from you than that simplistic, narrow-minded label."

I worked up some spit again. "Sorry to disappoint."

She said something in French then.

"What? Oh. You're speaking in French again. Am I supposed to be impressed?"

My testicles ascended when I felt a gentle pressure on my throat. I backed away, but didn't escape it. I gagged.

It stopped.

"Do I have to get nasty? You might show a little respect. You may not know what I am, but you know enough about me by now to know you should probably show me a little fucking *respect*."

I coughed and stammered. "I-I-I'm sorry. I mean, I mean, I-I'm—"

"Oh, shut up, please. You sound so pathetic. It's people like you, Ryan, who make me wonder why I even bother. You know what I mean? I give and I give, and what kind of appreciation do I get? 'Are you a demon?' Really, can't you do better than that? Why don't you go now, Ryan. You're beginning to bore me. You wouldn't like me when I'm bored, trust me."

I gulped. This wasn't going well at all.

"You know, your mother doesn't have long to go, Ryan," the thing said. "Here, I'll show you."

I'm still trying to get over what happened next.

Maddy's bedroom melted away like ice cream under a hot blowdryer. I found myself standing in a small, dark, dingy room furnished with a bed, and a round table and chair over by the window, with a small television on the table, an ugly swag lamp hanging above it. The room smelled of cigarettes and body odor. The walls were yellow from cigarette smoke, the curtains a drab tan color. The brown carpet was ratty and had holes in it here and there. Some dull yellow light came from a small lamp on the nightstand beside the bed, but it wasn't much.

The bed's covers were tangled up at the foot of the bed and Phyllis was stretched out on it in her bra and panties, on her back. She looked like a corpse, all bones under a paper-thin layer of pale bruised skin. She lay still with her mouth wide open and her eyes closed.

On the nightstand beside the bed next to the small lamp, I saw a spoon, a Zippo cigarette lighter, and a hypodermic.

I stood there for what seemed a long time, and I wondered if she was already dead. But I could see that she was breathing, although barely. Then her body convulsed once, twice. She vomited, and some of it spurted up from her mouth, dribbled over the corners and ran down her cheeks. But most of it stayed in her mouth. She made a gurgling sound then, and convulsed some more. Then she stopped breathing.

I was back in Maddy's bedroom and she grinned at me.

"Unfortunate, isn't it?" the thing said. "The doctors call it aspiraiton. And it's going to happen soon. But then, you don't care, do you?"

I realized tears were running down my face. My throat was hot and a sob worked its way up from deep in my chest.

"Why did you shuh-show me that?" I said.

"Why not? Now, what shall I show you next? I know—how about your *own* death, Ryan? I'll show you how *you* are going to die, how about that?"

I couldn't get out of that room fast enough. I stumbled and fell going up the basement stairs. I came upstairs to the bathroom and then here, to my bedroom.

I can't stop shaking.

All of a sudden, I find myself wanting to see Phyllis. Wanting to see my mom. Just one more time before she chokes to death on her own vomit in that awful little motel room. I've never felt anything for her before—well, never anything good, anyway. But now, I feel so sad for her, it hurts. It hurts in the pit of my stomach.

I know there's no way I'll get to sleep. It's one-thirty in the morning, but I'm going to sneak out of the house and go see Mr. Granger. I don't want to be alone right now, I need to talk to someone.

And I don't want to be in the same house with that thing.

SEVEN

Elliott had just gone to bed when his doorbell rang. He got up in T-shirt and boxer shorts, put on his robe, and pushed his walker down the hall to the living room, to the front door. He let Ryan in.

The boy looked terrified. His eyes were wide and he was pale, mouth open. He had difficulty stringing words together into a sentence at first. Elliott put a kettle of water on the stove to make tea and tried to calm Ryan down.

Ryan paced the living room. When he finally started talking clearly, he told Elliott what had just happened in the basement bedroom, told him about seeing his mother die.

"That thing was going to show me how *I'm* gonna die then," he said. "So I got the hell out of there." He took the tape recorder from his shirt pocket and handed it to Elliott. "Here. It said something in French again."

Elliott listened to the tape.

Hearing that deep whisky-voice again gave him a chill. When he got to the line in French, he stopped the tape and rewound it a bit, then picked up the phone on the endtable beside his recliner and called Francis Feighan.

"Who's this?"

"Hi, Francis. I hope I didn't wake you."

"No, I'm up. Sounds like we have a better connection this time."

"Listen to this."

He put the recorder up to the receiver and played it: "*Comment vous m'aiment casser l'autre hanche, abruti?*" He turned off the recorder.

Francis laughed. "Are you ever going to explain all this?"

"Later, Francis. What's the translation?"

"'How would you like me to break the other hip, idiot?' That's the translation."

Elliott dropped the recorder into his lap. His mouth was suddenly dry and his heart was beating faster.

"Thank you, Francis," he said. "I've got to go."

"Hey, what's going on, anyway?"

"Later. I'll tell you later. 'Bye." He punched the Off button and returned the phone to its base.

"What did it mean?" Ryan said as he finally sat on the couch.

Elliott told him.

They sat in silence for awhile, with their own thoughts.

Elliott was scared.

"Have you told her ... it ... about me?" Elliot said.

"No. I haven't even mentioned you."

But it knows about my hip, Elliott thought. *And it knew about the bad connection on the line when I was talking to Francis yesterday, before it even happened.*

He leaned forward with his elbows on his thighs and put his face in his hands. He jumped when the kettle whistled. He pushed his walker into the kitchen and put tea bags into two mugs, poured the water. He had Ryan carry the mugs out to the living room. They said nothing, just sat there while their tea steeped.

Elliott played the tape again. His heart broke when he heard Maddy say, "Help me, Ryan. Please help me." She sounded so sad and hopeless.

"What if it's serious?" Ryan whispered in a harsh rasp.

"About what?"

"It said now that it told me, it would have to kill me."

"It could've killed you right then and there if it wanted to. I'm sure if it wanted you dead, you would be by now." But Elliott had little confidence in his words. He knew he was incapable of predicting what this thing would or wouldn't do. He'd never written any fiction about possession, so he'd never researched it. All he knew was what he'd gotten from the fiction he'd read and the movies he'd seen, and he knew how unreliable that could be.

"We'll talk to Marie tomorrow," Elliott said. "Maybe we can convince her to involve her minister."

"You think she needs to be exorcised?" Ryan said.

"What do you think, Ryan?"

After a long moment, Ryan nodded. "Yeah. You're right." He thought a moment, then said, "What about her?"

"Maddy."

"Yeah. You heard her. She asked me to help her. She's trapped in there somewhere with that thing."

Elliott took in a deep breath and sighed. "You go ahead and drink your tea, Ryan, calm yourself down. When you're feeling better, go back home to bed. In the morning, we'll talk to Marie. If there's some way we can help Maddy, we will."

"I don't know if I can sleep over there anymore," Ryan said.

"Like I said, if it was going to kill you, it probably would have by now."

But Elliott did not know that to be true. He wasn't even in the same house with the thing, and he felt unsafe.

He had the unnerving feeling that somehow it was watching every move he made.

EIGHT

Elliott woke the next morning to the sound of his doorbell ringing. It was only a few minutes after eight. He got up and put on his robe, pushed his walker out to the living room, and let Ryan in.

"I sneaked out right after breakfast," Ryan said. "Before they could assign me any chores. Are we going to call Marie now?"

"Whoa," Elliott said, his eyes half-open. "I've gotta have coffee first. Then we'll call Marie."

Elliott made some coffee and they sat at the kitchen table drinking it in silence. He wondered if Ryan was thinking about the thing, too.

Of course he is, Elliott thought. *It's all he can think about, just like it's all I can think about.*

Ryan had stayed until after three that morning. They'd watched old sitcoms on Nick at Nite while they drank their tea. They hadn't said much, although a great deal of unspoken things hovered in the air between them—things about the girl in the basement next door.

After drinking a couple cups of coffee, Elliott rubbed his eyes with the heels of his hands, and said, "Okay. I'll give her a call."

He called Marie and asked her to please come over and help him with something. She was at the door five minutes later with a plate of persimmon cookies for him. Her smile faltered slightly when she saw Ryan.

"I didn't expect to see you here, Ryan," she said. "I didn't even know you'd left the house yet."

Elliott said, "Ryan and I would like to have a word with you, Marie."

"About what?" she said.

"Why don't you come have a seat," he said, leading her to the kitchen table. "Would you like a cup of coffee?"

She frowned slightly, but her smile never went away entirely. "Is something wrong, Mr. Granger?"

"Please call me Elliott, Marie. Sit down. Please."

He poured her a cup of coffee, then poured more coffee into his own cup and Ryan's. He sat down first, and Marie followed. She put the cookies on the table. Ryan got the microcassette recorder on the endtable beside the recliner and brought it over to the table. He sat down across from Elliott.

"Marie, I'd like to talk to you about Maddy," Elliott said.

Marie's smile disappeared, her back stiffened, and a hand went to her mouth. "Oh, I can't talk about Maddy," she said abruptly.

Elliott said, "Why can't you talk about her, Marie?"

"Well, because there are privacy issues ... I'm not allowed to just ... I can't go around ... "

"Who were those people who came to the house yesterday?" Elliott asked. "I know they were there to see Maddy. Who were they?"

Marie looked at Ryan a moment, then turned to Elliott. Her smile was gone, her face firm. "What's going on here, Mr. Granger?"

"All I want you to do, Marie, is listen to Ryan and me for a few minutes, all right?" Elliott said.

"About what? What's going *on* here?" She was frustrated and a little angry.

Elliott said, "Ryan has been talking to Maddy lately, Marie, and he's recorded his conversations with her. I don't think you know what you've got in that basement of yours, and I think you should know. Do you know what's wrong with Maddy, Marie?"

"She has multiple-personality disorder," Marie said. "She's a very disturbed little girl. But she's generally well-behaved." As she said this, the corners of Marie's mouth pulled back and her eyes crinkled up and she looked like she was about to cry.

"Do you really believe that?" Elliott said.

"It's what they told me."

"Those people in the suits?"

She nodded.

"Listen to this recording. It covers two separate conversations Ryan had with Maddy."

Elliott nodded at Ryan and he started the tape.

As Marie listened, tears welled up in her eyes. Elliott gestured for Ryan to get her a paper towel from the roll over the counter, and he did. She dabbed at her eyes as she cried silently. Before the tape was finished, she said, "All right, all right, I've heard enough. What did you think you were accomplishing by doing this, Ryan?"

Elliott reached over and stopped the tape.

Ryan said, "I just wanted to meet her at first, to talk to her. I figured she must get lonely down there in that basement room, and there was no rule that we weren't allowed to talk to Maddy. So I went down and saw her. And she talked to me in that voice. She said things in French. And if you want to know the truth, Marie, she scared the hell out of me because she knew something about me no one could possibly know—that I want to be a writer. No one knew that."

"Well, I could've guessed it," Marie said. "More than once, I've found you writing at the kitchen table in the middle of the night."

"Yes, but did you tell Maddy that?"

Her face scrunched up again and she shed more tears. She sucked her lips in between her teeth and pressed the wadded up paper towel over her mouth.

"Marie, what do you know about Maddy?" Elliott said.

"Just what I told you. She has multiple personality disorder. They told me to keep her out of the general population of the house, to keep her in her room except for a period of exercise every day. They ... I shouldn't be telling you this."

"Why not?"

"Because they ... they told me not to tell anyone."

"Marie, doesn't it make you a little suspicious that people in government cars and black suits are telling you not to tell anyone about a girl in your care?"

She took a couple deep breaths, then sipped her coffee. "We only had swamp coolers in the house, and the summers here are *so* hot. They put in central air and heat for us. They had the house repainted for us. They put in the pool. They said they wanted to make the house the best possible place to live for the children we cared for. All they asked is that we keep Maddy under wraps. They didn't want her to mingle with the others."

"Why didn't you tell us that?" Ryan asked. "If I'd known I wasn't *supposed* to talk to Maddy, I might not have done it."

Marie shrugged. "I thought it would be best if I just said nothing about it. I was afraid if I made it a rule, then you kids would be doing it all the time, just to be getting away with something. I've been taking care of foster kids most of my life, I know how they are. So I said nothing, and the other kids just ignored her. Once in awhile, I'll have one of the girls help me dress Maddy, because she's so big and unwieldy, but they never really interact with her. So, it worked, my plan worked. At least, it worked until now." She turned to Ryan.

Elliott said, "Marie, didn't you notice there was something strange about Maddy?"

"Of *course* I did," she said, and she started crying again. She dabbed at her eyes some more. "The things she says ... and that voice ... but I had no reason not to believe them. They told me her behavior would be strange. Even frightening. They said at times, she might sound like another person. And she *does*. That voice she speaks in sometimes ... it *is* frightening."

Ryan said, "Has it ever said anything to you that's ... personal? Something no one else would know about you?"

"It? You're talking about Maddy, now?"

"No, I'm talking about the thing that talks through Maddy," Ryan said.

Marie froze with her eyes on Ryan. Her hand was halfway from the table to her face holding the wadded-up paper towel. Her eyes were widened slightly and her lips parted, and she looked as if she'd just been slapped. Suddenly, she stood.

"I can't talk about this anymore," she said.

"Marie, I think you should," Elliott said. He reached out and took her hand. "I'm not accusing you of anything, Marie, so please don't feel defensive. You were given this girl to take care of, and you've taken care of her. You've taken good care of her, I'm sure. But we need to discuss the thing that's talking through her. I find it hard to believe that you don't know about it, that you haven't had some experience with it."

Marie slowly lowered herself back into the chair. She took her hand from Elliott's and put it on the table.

"My mother was murdered," she said. "She lived down in the Bay Area, in Redwood City. She moved down there to live with her sister, who wasn't well and needed help getting around. One night, a man broke into the house as she was getting ready to go to bed. My aunt was already in bed asleep, but Mom was still up, and this guy broke in, and he stabbed her to death. He was a serial killer. He'd killed three others before her, and he killed two others after her. He'd break into houses at night and just kill people. Stab them to death. He usually caught them in their sleep. He left Aunt Fiona alone, but he raped and killed my mother. That's what else he did to the people in the houses he broke into at night—he raped the women, sometimes the little girls."

Elliott nodded once. "I remember it in the news. Back in the early eighties."

"There was one detail the police never released to the media," Marie said. "The killer always carved a cross in the victims' abdomens. They left that detail out so they'd be able to separate the nutcases who confess to everything under the sun from the real guy, if he should decide to confess. It was the one detail only the killer would know. But he never confessed. And they never found him. The killings stopped. Some think he moved, others think he died, and others think he just stopped and went back to his probably perfectly normal life."

Elliott had a pretty good idea where Marie's story was going, and he didn't like it.

"But Maddy knew," she whispered. "One day, I was walking her around the backyard and she turned to me and said, 'The man who killed your mother is dead.' She said it in that horrible voice, that deep, rough voice. 'He got hit by a car while crossing the street,' she said. 'That's why the killings stopped and they never found him,' she said. Then she stopped walking and turned to me and smiled, and I smiled back because it was such a big smile, I thought she was going to say something nice, or laugh, or something. Instead, she said in that voice, she said, 'Your mother suffered, you know. She was still alive when he carved that cross into her belly. He did that because he was messed up by religious-fanatic parents, you know. They made him that way. They made him that way in the name of God. Why do you suppose your God lets things like that happen, Marie? And in His name? Why do you suppose that is?' And I swear, I wanted so badly to slap that girl's face. I wanted to do it so much, I could already feel the sting on my palm. But I've never raised my hand to any of the kids in my care, and I wasn't about to start with a mentally-handicapped girl like Maddy. The problem was, I believed her somehow. When she talked in that voice, I knew what she was saying was true, and I believed it. But I took her hand and kept walking, and I just wouldn't respond. She kept trying to get me to respond, but I wouldn't do it. I just wouldn't. And I still won't. I just don't listen to it. I tune it out. I don't have to have much contact with her, anyway, so I just put up with it and try to think of other things."

A sob quaked Marie and Ryan got her another paper towel. She buried her face in it and cried.

Elliott reached over and put a hand on her shoulder, gave it a squeeze. "I'm sorry for upsetting you, Marie, but I don't think it's a good idea to ignore this. Have you thought about poor Maddy?"

"What *about* Maddy?" she said. "I take very good care of that girl."

"I'm sure you do, Marie, but think about it. You just said you don't have to have much contact with her—you don't like to be around her, and I don't blame you. But the reason you don't like being around her has nothing to do with the girl herself. It's the thing that's talking through her. Maddy is a nine-year-old girl who needs care and affection. The thing that's inside her—"

"I told you, she has multiple personality—"

"How do you explain the fact that it knew about the cross in those killings?" Elliott said. "That's not multiple-personality disorder, Marie, that's something supernatural at work."

Elliott told her of the thing's recorded comment about the bad connection on the line when he called Francis, and about its remark about breaking his *other* hip.

"Have you told Maddy about my hip, Marie?"

"Of course not."

"Then how did she know about it? Marie, you're a religious woman, aren't you?"

"I go to church. My faith is very important to me. It's gotten me through some pretty hard times."

"I was raised a Christian," Elliott said. "I haven't been to church in a long time, but it's not the kind of thing you just stop believing. And if you want to know the truth, I've been feeling some of it coming back on me in the last couple days." He glanced at the microcassette recorder on the table. "Whatever it is that knew about your mother's killer and knew about my hip, it scares the hell out of me, Marie. And it's *using* Maddy. It sounds like this poor girl is being held captive by this *thing*."

"You heard her when she asked me for help," Ryan said. He frowned at his coffee as he remembered it, then looked at Marie. "She sounded so sad and afraid. I don't think she understands what's happening to her. Who knows what that thing is doing to her."

Marie finished her coffee and stood. She took the cup to the sink and washed it out, then put it on the counter. "What do you want from me?" she said.

"We have to do something to help that girl," Elliott said. "What's your church's stand on exorcism, Marie?"

Marie turned around and her mouth opened and closed like the mouth of a desperate fish flopping on land. Finally, she said, "What are you talking about?"

Elliott said, "I thought you could have your minister come see her. Maybe there's some kind of ceremony—"

"Hank would never allow it," she said.

"How can he *not* allow it, Marie?" Elliott said.

"You haven't been around those people." She paced the kitchen for several seconds, then sat down at the table again and leaned toward Elliott. "You know how, when you go to the dentist, he's nice and pleasant when he first comes in, asks how you are, that sorta thing, then, bam, he's all business and you're just a mouth as far as he's concerned. Well, it's funny, but these people remind me of dentists. They come in, they're all nicey-nice, and then, bam, they're all business and I feel like I'm nothing but a mouth to them, somebody they've gotta respond to to be polite. All they care about is Maddy. They told me she was part of some study, that they were giving her a new drug. I have to give her pills twice a day, and I have to make sure she swallows them. They spend hours with her. Once, they came early in the morning and they stayed late into the night, and they set up this satellite link-up equipment in Maddy's bedroom. I don't know what it was for because they wouldn't let us stick around to find out. We had to go back upstairs and keep everyone out of the basement. They're not the kind of people you say no to. They're the kind of people whose orders you tend to follow, too, and I'm going to be in big trouble if they find out about you two."

Elliott shook his head. "Marie, don't worry about that. Ryan and I are going to keep this to ourselves, right Ryan?" He turned to Ryan, who nodded. "This is just between the three of us, Marie. I bring it up because I'm not sure you fully understand what you've got in your basement."

She frowned. It was not an expression often seen on Marie's face, and it made her look very unlike herself. "You're not sure I ... what, I don't understand."

"That's what worries me. Marie, you seem to be clinging to the idea that Maddy is just suffering from multiple-personality disorder, from some mental illness, when it's pretty obvious to me that she is possessed by some entity, some being. Ryan and I have come to the conclusion that it is not a friendly or moral being, and frankly, it scares the hell out of us. Do you understand what I'm saying? Those people have been lying to you."

Marie put a thick elbow on the table and slowly rubbed her hand down over her face. "It's always trying to get me to doubt my faith," she said after a long silence. "I usually hum to myself when it starts to talk to me. When it's just Maddy, it's fine. She can be such a sweet girl, you know, she's very good-natured. When it's her. But it's not always her. On those days, I hum a lot and try not to hear all the terrible things it says about God and Jesus. They're terrible things, but later, they nag at me, the things it says. I have to pray a lot to get it out of my head, but that's getting difficult to do. I can only hum so much. Some of that stuff ... it gets through. I hate it for that, for doing that to me, for making me question my own faith, the faith that's saved my life more than once. I hate it for that."

Elliott frowned. "So you've known all along."

She rested the side of her head in her hand. "I've suspected. But it's not the kind of suspicion you share with anyone. People would say I was crazy, and I'm half afraid they might be right. But I'll tell you right now, I don't think it would matter one bit to Hank. Even if I could convince him, I don't think he'd care, as long as all the nice stuff keeps coming in. He probably wouldn't care if she was possessed by Satan and the ghost of Elvis, as long as those people keep doing things like painting our house and installing central air and heat and putting in a pool, and bringing in that big-screen TV with all that sound equipment, all that stuff. That's why the idea of calling in Reverend Tomlin would never work. What would be the purpose? To get rid of it, right? Do you know what kind of trouble we'd be in if we got rid of that thing, Mr. Granger? Like I said, you don't know what these people are like. They're all business right down to their souls, they don't *have* anything else in them."

Elliott noticed a change in Marie's features—they all seemed to collapse a little as if beneath some great inner weight.

Ryan said, "But I don't understand, how can you live knowing that thing is under the same roof with you?"

The rest of Marie seemed to collapse a little then, and she was overtaken by sobs. Elliott could tell that taking care of Maddy had been taking a toll on Marie, and he suspected this was the first time she'd expressed it.

Her upper body rocked back and forth slightly as she cried. "It's been awful. Hank doesn't know. He never sees her. He doesn't have anything to do with her. Hank has no idea what it's like."

"Maybe it's time to show him, Marie," Elliott said. "Maybe it's time you show Hank what you've been dealing with."

"I've tried, I've tried. When I take Maddy for her walk, sometimes Hank is out in the backyard, and I'll take her over to him. She's fine then. She always says, 'Hi, Hank,' and, ''Bye, Hank.' She's always just fine with him."

Elliott felt a great wave of affection for Marie. She had enough on her hands taking care of six problematic teenage boys and girls— she didn't need an other-worldly entity in her house chipping away at her faith. He sensed she didn't get much help from Hank. But she endured and did her job with great care. She didn't deserve to have something like that in her life.

"Marie, you've got to call in your reverend," Elliott said. "Just have him spend some time with her, see what happens. Have him pray with her."

She dabbed at her eyes and cheeks with the paper towel, then looked at Elliott. Her puffy face was flatly expressionless. "Do you think that would be a good idea?" she said.

"I think you owe it to Maddy," Elliott said. "Can you imagine how she must feel? She's not in control of herself anymore. Who knows if she ever was entirely in control. Don't you know anything about her, Marie?"

She blew her nose as delicately as she could, then shook her head. "Only what those dentist people told me. They said her mother was a drug addict, father unknown, and that because of her multiple-personality disorder, she was part of a government study involving certain new medications. They come once a month to spend time alone with her. They always have video equipment. If they were to come and that ... that person, that thing, whatever it is, if it were gone ... I don't even like to think about it."

"How would they know you had anything to do with it?" Ryan said.

"Well, they would ask, I'm sure," Marie said.

"And you could lie to them," Ryan said.

"Oh, no. I couldn't lie. It's not just that it's wrong, I really can't lie—I'm a terrible liar."

"How do you know Reverend—what's his name again?" Elliott said.

"Reverend Tomlin."

"We don't even know if Reverend Tomlin can get rid of this thing," Elliott said. "Just bring him over to see her, Marie. See what he has to say about her. I think someone like a minister or a priest needs to see her. And I think you owe it to Maddy, Marie."

Marie got up and took her coffee mug from the counter, went to the coffee maker and poured more. She took it to the table and sat down again, sipped it.

"I can ask him over to pray for her," she said. "That wouldn't seem unusual, and it would be a chance for him to spend some time with her. But that's no guarantee that voice is gonna say anything."

"It can't hurt to try," Elliott said. "You'll do this, then?"

She sipped the coffee. "I'll call Reverend Tomlin this morning."

Elliott smiled and exchanged a satisfied look with Ryan.

Marie turned to Ryan and said, "But you've got to leave Maddy alone, Ryan. And you can't tell *any* of the others about this. Do you understand me?"

Ryan said, "Yes, I understand, I won't tell anyone. But you've got to let me be there when the minister comes."

She started to protest, but thought about it another moment. "We'll see," she said.

"Would you do me a favor, Marie?" Ryan said. "Would you drive me over to see my mom before I have to go to work? She's staying at a motel in Anderson."

"Sure, I can do that, Ryan."

He smiled. "Thanks."

From the Journal of Ryan Kettering

I saw Phyllis today. Marie took me. She said she'd wait in the car while I went to see my mom. I told her she didn't have to, but she said that was okay, she would.

The Lazy Z Ranch Motel was once painted a chocolate-brown with mint-green trim, but the paint is all faded and peeling now. The doors of most of the bungalows were open and people were sitting outside in the shade of their small covered porches. Cars were parked in front of some of them, all old cars, mostly banged up and gnarly-looking. I didn't know which bungalow Phyllis was in, so I went up to this hugely fat old woman with no teeth seated outside her bungalow reading a tabloid and asked for Phyllis Kettering.

"Oh, Phyl'th jutht down the way there in number five," the woman said.

Phyllis had her door open and *The Jerry Springer Show* (what could be more appropriate?) was playing loudly on a small black-and-white TV with rabbit-ears. She sat in a chair just inside with her back to me, smoking a cigarette. She jittered and fidgeted as she watched the television. She wore the same red halter top and jeans she'd worn when she came to see me. Her legs were propped up on the round table beneath the front window, her feet, in sandals, just a few inches from the television. She had an iced drink on the table near a half-full bottle of whiskey. A swag lamp hung over the table. I knocked on the doorjamb and said, "Hello."

She jolted out of the chair and turned on me so suddenly, I thought she was going to attack me, and I took a step back.

"Baby!" she gasped. "You came to see me!" She dropped her cigarette into the ashtray on the table, rushed forward, and threw her arms around me. She smelled of liquor. For a second, I thought she was going to pick me up off the ground, but she didn't have the strength in her to do that. As she hung onto me and I embraced her in return, all I felt were bones.

With my head on her shoulder, I looked around the small, dingy room and all the air was sucked out of my lungs for a few seconds. It was the same room the thing in Maddy had shown me. The same room I'd seen Phyllis die in—the same chair and table, the same bed, the same lamp, the same ratty brown carpet.

Phyllis pushed me back and looked into my eyes for several seconds. It was the longest she'd done that in ... well, as long as I can remember. "You gonna come meet my friends? C'mon."

She put her arm around my shoulders and led me out of the bungalow, down to the fat old woman I'd talked to on the way in.

"Miriam, I want you to meet my handsome boy," Phyllis said. "Ain't he a handsome fella?"

"Why, he sure ith," Miriam said with a toothless grin. "I wondered when I theen him if he wath yourth."

"Oh, c'mon, c'mon, you gotta meet Gus." She took me across the small courtyard. In the center of it stood an old fountain swallowed up by ivy. Gus's door was open and Phyllis walked me right in without knocking. Gus was a scrawny guy with buck teeth who sat on the edge of his bed, smoking and drinking a bottle of beer. He wore a tanktop and baggy tan shorts. His arms and legs were blue with tattoos. When Phyllis introduced me, he stood and shook my hand. He was missing a couple fingers.

"Gladda meetcha, Ryan," he said, and his breath reeked of beer. He swayed a bit as he stood in front of me. "Your mom's good people, Ryan, real good people."

Next, she took me to meet Glynnis, a young woman in shorts and a T-shirt whose bungalow smelled of marijuana. Glynnis didn't say much, just laughed quietly and nodded a lot.

Then Phyllis took me back to her bungalow, saying, "I got cookies in my room, and some juice. Would you like to have some cookies and juice with me?"

As she walked beside me, her arm across my shoulders, she seemed to bounce along to a beat only she could hear. Back in her room, she pushed me down in the chair and went to the tiny kitchenette. There was a small green refrigerator on the counter and she opened it and removed a bottle of grapejuice, got a couple glasses from the cupboard, and poured. She took a package of Chips Ahoy cookies from the cupboard and put them on the table

by my chair. She handed me the juice, then sat on the edge of the
bed facing me.

"Oh, I'm so happy you came t'see me, honey," she said. "Did you
ride your bike over?" She took a drink of her juice, then set it down
on the floor.

"No, Marie brought me. She's waiting in her car."

"She didn't have to wait."

"She wanted to. I think so we could be alone."

"Well, that was nice of her. You'll have to take her some cookies."
She crossed her right leg over her left and her right foot bounced
up and down.

I felt very uncomfortable being in the room. I had a dizzying
sense of *deja vu*. She was sitting on the same bed she would die on
soon.

"Look, um ... Mom." I hadn't called her Mom since I was a little
kid, and it felt odd coming out of my mouth. "When you came to
see me, you said you were clean."

"I am. I been clean. Sixteen days, clean as a whistle. Well, 'cept
for drinkin', I been drinkin' a little, but no drugs."

"Well, I'm not sure I believe you. But if you are, you've got to
stay that way. Do you hear me?"

"Well, sure, honey."

"No, I mean this, it's important." I leaned forward in the chair
and put an elbow on the table. "You can't do anymore drugs,
because if you do, it's going to kill you. Do you understand?"

She got up and went to the table, got her cigarette from the
ashtray. It had gone out, so she picked up her Zippo and relit it. She
took the ashtray to the bed with her. She dragged on the cigarette
and blew the smoke out hard as she sat down on the edge of the
bed again. Her expression hardened.

"Zat why you come over here?" she said. "To preach at me?"

"No, I'm not preaching. I'm just worried about you, is all."

"Look, I know I gotta problem. Okay? But I'm dealin' with it. I
go to my meetings."

I smiled. "That's good! That's great! Just keep it up, that's all I'm
saying. I'm just worried about what'll happen to you if you ... you
know, if you ... relapse."

"Well, I ain't *gonna* relapse, dammit."

"Okay."

"I don't need you comin' over here tellin' me about the dangers a drugs, dammit."

"Okay. I didn't mean to—"

"You think you're tellin' me somethin' I don't know?"

"No, I was—"

"Get out."

"No, wait, Mom, please, I just wanted to—"

"You heard me. Get out."

"No, I don't want to—"

"I give you juice and cookies and you start in on me like some kinda fuckin' preacher."

"Please don't do this."

She stood up and waved toward the open door. "Get out. Now."

My throat burned and tears stung my eyes. Where had I gone wrong? How had this gone so bad so suddenly? I stood and stepped toward her.

"Please, Mom, I just wanted to see you—"

"You just wanted to come over and preach at me. Well, take it somewheres else, 'cause I don't fuckin' need it."

"Can't we just—"

"*Go*, I said!" she shouted through clenched teeth. "Get *out*, dammit!" Her eyes were wide and her face trembled.

I backed away from her.

"Go!"

I turned and left the room. As I walked away, I heard her still talking.

"I don't need nobody preachin' t'me about the dangers of fuckin' drugs, 'specially some teenage punk."

I looked back one time, but saw only the open door. She was inside.

I know I won't see her again. Not alive, anyway. That's why I went—I wanted to see her one last time. I probably shouldn't have said anything about the drugs, but I thought if I warned her, I might be able to keep it from happening. Or at least hold it off for awhile longer.

I probably shouldn't have said anything. But how could I not?

I didn't speak as Marie drove me back home. I spent the time trying not to cry.

As we were pulling into the driveway, Marie said, "I called Reverend Tomlin on my cellphone while you were seeing your mother, Ryan. He's going to come over this evening, after dinner. If you don't say anything to Hank or the others about it, and I mean not a *word*, then I'll try to take you downstairs to Maddy's room with us. But only if I can do it without Hank noticing, because he'd think that was odd. Okay?"

I nodded. "Okay."

I've got to get ready for work now, but I don't feel like it. All I can think about is my mother lying in that lonely room, choking to death on her own vomit.

NINE

Reverend Joseph Tomlin was a tall man in his mid-fifties with a narrow, weary face. His wavy dark hair was cut very short and was shot through with streaks of white. He wore small round glasses and a dark blue suit, and he carried a bible bound in rich wine-colored leather under his right arm.

He went into the living room first and talked with Marie and Hank. Everyone was down in the rec room playing games, and they'd invited over some friends from up the street to show off the new stuff in the rec room. Once he saw that they were going to be awhile, Ryan went downstairs, too, and played a couple video games with Gary and Keith. After awhile, he went back upstairs. Marie, Hank, and Reverend Tomlin were still in the living room talking, but the reverend was standing now.

Reverend Tomlin said, "We would love to have you at church sometime, Hank."

Smiling, Hank stood and said, "Well, it's a pleasure to meet you, Reverend, and I mean no offense, but that just ain't gonna happen. I'm not the church-goin' type, I'm afraid. Although I wouldn't mind showing up for a pot luck now and then, I got nothing against good food."

Ryan went through the living room and dining room to the kitchen and got a drink of water. Then he went down the hall and waited at the top of the basement stairs. In a few minutes, Marie came down the hall with Reverend Tomlin. She introduced Ryan and they shook hands, then they went downstairs. They turned left at the bottom and went to Maddy's room. Marie knocked a couple times, then pushed it open and said, "Hi, Maddy, honey. You have a visitor."

She stepped aside and let Tomlin and Ryan come in.

Maddy sat on the floor playing with some of her toys. She got to her feet with a little effort and turned to face them.

"Hello, Ryan," she said in her normal voice.

"Hi, Maddy," he said with a smile.

"Maddy, this is Reverend Tomlin from church," Marie said. "He came to meet you and pray with you. Isn't that nice?"

Maddy looked at Ryan and a sneer passed over her lips as she rolled her eyes. "Oh, very fucking funny," she said in the deep, smoky voice.

Tomlin frowned and Marie gasped.

"*Maddy!*" she said. "We do *not* talk like that in this house!" She turned to the reverend. "I'm *so* sorry, Reverend Tomlin. I've *never* heard her use language like that before."

"Don't worry about it, Marie, I understand," he said, patting her shoulder.

Maddy went to her bed and sat on the edge of the mattress.

"Haven't you told him yet?" Ryan said.

Marie looked at him and shook her head—it was not a response to Ryan's question, but a signal for him to say no more.

"But he has to know," Ryan said. He turned to Tomlin. "This girl is possessed, Reverend Tomlin. There's something inside her that doesn't belong there, something evil. You just heard it. Didn't you hear her voice?"

"Oh, please," the voice said. Maddy leaned back on her arms, elbows locked, and looked the reverend up and down with an expression of disgust on her fat face. "What do you expect me to do now, Ryan, vomit pea soup and talk dirty?"

Tomlin's chin dropped.

"What are *you* looking at?" it said to Tomlin. "You take that Bible with you when you go to fuck those lonely wives in your congregation, Reverend? Huh? Yes you do, don't deny it. You like to read aloud from the Book of Revelation while they suck on your noodle, don't you?"

Tomlin dropped his Bible as he stumbled backward and slapped a hand over his mouth—his hand actually made a loud *smack* sound when it hit.

Marie stood with her mouth hanging open. She looked first at Maddy, then turned to Tomlin.

"Your wife didn't like it," Maddy went on. "It gave her the creeps to hear you reading from the Bible during sex. But your devoted followers, your lonely housewife groupies, they get off on it, don't they? They find it so delightfully *kinky*. And it is, by the way. You know, you're a bit of a nutcase, Joe, and you'll probably never be able to afford the amount of therapy you need, but you're okay by me, because you so beautifully illustrate what I always say, and what I always say is, *nobody* can get through life following *His* stupid rules. So why bother trying? In fact, why not go so far as to use your position as one of His representantives to get some nooky. Right, Joe?"

"Oh, my God," Tomlin said into his hand with a sob.

Maddy looked at Marie, whose jaw was slack as she looked at the reverend.

"How about that, Marie?" she said. "Your beloved Reverend Tomlin, the man you've admired so much for so long, is actually diddling several wives in the church. All at the same time, too. To look at him, you wouldn't think he had it in him, would you? But he's a very busy minister."

Marie looked at Tomlin as if he had just personally insulted her.

"Look at me, Marie," the voice said.

Marie turned her head and looked at Maddy.

"Are you going to put up with that?" it said. "After all the time and effort you've put into his church? After the faith and trust you've put in him over the years? Only to find out he's just another huckster lookin' to get laid? Are you going to take that in stride? Are you going to put up with that?"

Ryan flinched when he heard Marie growl. It was a sound low in her throat and it came out as she turned and pounced on the reverend. With her hands on his throat, her lips peeled back over her clenched teeth in a hideous smile that sent a shudder through Ryan's shoulders. Tomlin gurgled as she slammed him against the wall and squeezed his throat.

Ryan grabbed her shoulders from behind, pulled her away from the reverend, and got her hands off his throat, but she kept lurching toward him again each time he let go of her. Ryan got in front of her and pushed her across the room until her back was against the dresser. She fought with him. Finally, she groped for *his* throat. Ryan slapped her hard in the face.

Marie gasped and pulled away from him. Her eyes grew large as realization settled over her face, as she became fully aware of exactly what she had been doing seconds ago. She turned and hurried to Tomlin, who shrank away from her.

"I'm so sorry, Reverend Tomlin," she said as tears rolled from her eyes. "I wasn't—that wasn't me."

Tomlin nodded as he gently rubbed his throat. "I believe you, Marie. This is clearly some kind of—"

"Let me show you something, Reverend Tomlin," the voice said.

Tomlin stood up straight at the foot of the bed and all the color disappeared from his face as a grey pallor moved in. The features of his face began to pull backward, into an expression of fear—a fear so great, it was obviously painful to him, because there was pain in his eyes, Ryan could see it. In a trembling falsetto voice, he said, "Oh my God oh my God oh my God oh my God," and his voice got louder as he raised an arm in defense, until he was screaming the three words over and over.

The reverend fell silent and collapsed to the floor.

"Oh, no," Marie said as she got on her knees beside him. She felt his neck for a pulse. She looked up at Ryan and said, "I know CPR. You go call 911 and get an ambulance here fast."

Ryan left the bedroom. The noise level in the rec room was so high—sounds from the video games, the television with the volume up, voices talking and laughing—that no one had heard Tomlin in Maddy's bedroom. Ryan hurried upstairs and used the kitchen phone to call 911. When he was done, he went back downstairs to Maddy's room. Marie vigorously performed CPR on Tomlin.

Maddy remained seated on the edge of her bed. With a quiet chuckle, the voice said, "How was I supposed to know he had a heart condition? I mean, really, with all the women he's *shtupping*, how can he have a heart condition, right?"

"Damn you," Ryan muttered.

"Oh, don't get self-righteous with *me*, you pusillanimous little punk," the voice said. "Don't worry, your turn is coming. You saw that expression on the reverend's face just before he went down? You'll look that way in the end, too, Ryan, you wait and see."

Ryan felt an icy cold wash over him in the same way it did when he opened the refrigerator and stepped forward to browse the shelves. It made his skin feel tight on his body.

"You really thought you could rope some Sunday-morning pulpit jockey into *exorcising* me, Ryan?" the voice said. "Bring them on. Bring your priests and your rabbis, bring on your best. Bring them all on at once. They'll be so busy fighting over who gets to exorcise me and how, they won't pay any attention to me. Even if they did, though, they would all fail, Ryan, because they're weak, and I'm very strong. I am healthy and vibrant. I flourish, Ryan. This is my time. And—" The voice laughed. "—there's not a damned thing you can do about it."

At one-thirty in the morning, Ryan and Lyssa met in the upstairs hall and went down to the rec room. They didn't turn on any lights and used only Ryan's penlight for illumination. In the basement, they curled up on the couch in the dark and Ryan turned on the TV. He found an old black-and-white monster movie—a giant reptilian monster rampaged through a city, stomping buildings and cars and crowds of people with stop-motion jerkiness. Ryan and Lyssa cuddled as they watched the movie. They didn't talk for awhile. It was as if they were both afraid of what they would talk about.

Marie and Hank had fought after the ambulance left with Reverend Tomlin. Hank had been upset that Marie had taken him downstairs to see Maddy. Marie had replied, "Just because we're supposed to keep the girl isolated don't mean she doesn't deserve to be prayed over by a minister of God, does it?" And Hank had said, "Yes, it *does*, because Dr. Sempris specifically said she didn't want Maddy to interact with anyone, dammit!" It had gone on like that for awhile.

When Ryan finally spoke, it was in a whisper. "Marie said Reverend Tomlin was in Intensive Care at the hospital. He had a heart attack." Ryan thought of the look of terror on Tomlin's face before he collapsed. "I wonder what that thing showed him."

"What are you going to do now?" Lyssa said.

He shrugged. "There's nothing I *can* do."

"I'm afraid Marie will ask me to help her with Maddy again. I hope she doesn't. I don't want to get near that girl."

"I don't want to be in the same house with her, to tell you the truth."

"I don't either." She cuddled into the crook of his arm. "What're we going to do?"

"I don't—" Ryan stopped and listened. "Did you just hear something?"

"No."

"I thought I heard the stairs creak, like somebody came down here." He picked up the remote and turned off the television. He slumped down on the couch and pulled Lyssa down with him so no one could see them sitting there from the hallway. He touched his lips to her ear and whispered, "I think someone went into Maddy's room."

"Who would do that at this hour?"

"Marie, probably. Let's just wait here for awhile."

They sat in silence in the dark for what felt like a long time. Then Ryan heard Maddy's bedroom door open down the hall. It had a high, abrupt squeak when it was first opened, and he recognized the sound. It was repeated when the door was closed. The next sound he heard made him flinch.

Keith cleared his throat.

Ryan got to his feet and turned on his penlight as he hurried to the hallway. He found Keith approaching the stairs. Ryan shined the light in his face, and Keith held up a hand to block it.

"What were you doing in there?" Ryan said.

"Nunna your fuckin' business, man." He cleared his throat as he went up the stairs.

Ryan sent the narrow beam down the hall to Maddy's door. He could go ask the thing what Keith was doing in there. But it wouldn't necessarily tell him. And he no longer felt safe talking to it. He figured he was probably going to be staying away from Maddy from now on. He went back to the couch. He turned the television back on. The Army was firing on the monster now. He slumped back down on the couch with his arm around Lyssa.

"What the hell was Keith doing in Maddy's room?" he said.

Lyssa shook her head. "He's never shown any interest in Maddy at all. In fact, I've never known him to behave as if even knows she lives here. I mean, he doesn't even acknowledge her."

Ryan was bothered by Keith's angry response—*Nunna your fuckin' business, man.* It was completely unlike him. Keith had never been anything but affable around Ryan—around anyone, as far as Ryan knew.

"If he found out anything about Maddy," Lyssa said, "he didn't hear it from me, because I haven't told anyone."

Frowning, Ryan said, "He looked almost like he was walking in his sleep."

Lyssa brought a leg around and straddled Ryan's lap, facing him. "Let's forget about Maddy for awhile, okay?" She kissed him.

He put his arms around her and held her close. But even deep in the kiss, he was unable to forget about Maddy, about the thing inside her. It was just down the hall.

Ryan could not rid himself of the sense that it knew what they were doing, that it was watching their every move.

From the Journal of Ryan Kettering

I keep thinking about Phyllis. Waiting for the phonecall. For the sad look on Marie's face when she comes to tell me.

I wish I'd never gone down the basement hall to Maddy's room. I wish I'd never spoken to that girl. I wish I'd never come to this house. It's probably the best house I've ever been in, but I wish I'd never come to it, never seen it.

I've got that feeling you get when you think someone's staring at you, when you can feel their eyes on your back, and you turn around, and sure enough, someone was looking at you, and he turns away as soon as you see him. That's the feeling I've got now, all the time, and I can't get rid of it. It's the feeling that eyes are on me. Narrow, piggy-eyes above those fat, dimpled cheeks. Eyes without much intelligence of their own.

Tomorrow morning, I'll go see Mr. Granger.

All I want to do now is sleep. And I hope I don't dream.

TEN

The next morning, Ryan found himself alone in the bedroom with Keith while Gary took a shower.

"Hey," Ryan said, "what were you doing in the basement last night?"

One corner of Keith's mouth turned up. "What? What're you talkin' about, dude?"

"You were down in the basement last night around two in the morning. I saw you. You were in Maddy's room."

"*Maddy's* room?" Keith's smile disappeared and he frowned. "What the hell would I go *there* for? I wasn't down in the basement. You musta been dreamin', or somethin', dude, 'cause I haven't been down in the basement since before I went to bed last night, and even if I was, I sure as hell wouldn't be goin' into that retarded kid's bedroom, so don't be sayin' that, okay? I don't want you startin' no rumors."

Keith was aggravated by the question, so Ryan decided to say no more. But Keith's denial did not make him doubt what he had seen—Keith had been down in the basement in Maddy's room in the early morning hours. He remembered how he'd looked—dazed and distant, as if he were walking in his sleep.

"You ever walk in your sleep, Keith?" Ryan asked.

"Hell, no, I don't walk in my sleep, dude, whyn't you drop it, okay?"

"Okay, okay, sorry."

For some reason, Keith's denial made Ryan feel worse about it. It seemed Keith really believed he had not gone down in the basement the night before. But just because Keith wasn't aware of it didn't mean he hadn't done it. There was always the chance he'd been *called* down in the basement.

But why?

* * *

Elliott had not slept well at all the night before. He wondered how things had gone next door with Marie's reverend. He couldn't shake the feeling that he was being watched, that his every move was being scrutinized.

He went through his supernatural reference books and looked up everything he could find on demons and possession. Some of what he found was mildly encouraging. He was still poring over one of the books when the doorbell rang. He had anticipated it.

"Come on in!" he shouted. "It's unlocked!"

He heard the security door open, then close, heard Ryan's footsteps come down the hall.

"Pull up a chair," Elliott said. "I've been doing some reading. The good news is, the possessed person almost always comes through the experience unscathed. It's the people *around* the possessed person who get messed up. One theory behind why demons possess people is to instill hopelessness in those around them, to create chinks of doubt in their faith. That sounds exactly like what the thing has been trying to do to Marie."

"Have you read anything about how to get rid of them?" Ryan said.

"Exorcism seems to be the only way. It's usually performed by a Catholic priest. It seems the Catholics have a history of this sort of thing and they're a little better at it than the protestants, although I read of a couple protestant exorcisms, too. Another thing—demons lie. They mix lies with truth to confuse and frighten. That got me to thinking. The people who came to see Maddy yesterday were definitely from the government, but that stuff the thing told you about advising them about the war may not be true at all. Maybe they're just studying the thing, you know? Maybe they've got her tucked away in this house here so they can figure out what makes that thing tick."

"So it's not necessarily true that it's helping them with the war?" Ryan said. "That the bombs are sacrifices?"

"Not ... necessarily. But it's impossible for us to tell. Not without talking to those people ourselves, and that's not going to happen."

Ryan slumped in the chair. "I couldn't write last night. That's never happened to me before. I just scribbled out a few paragraphs.

I couldn't concentrate. Still can't. All I can think about is that thing. And I have the feeling that ... it's watching me."

"Me, too. But I think we may be giving it more power than it has. We've been spooked, Ryan. It's already frightened us, it's got us off-balance. That's what it wants."

They said nothing for a little while. Elliott continued to read in the open book on the desk before him.

"I went to see my mom," Ryan said. "I wanted to see her before ... I mean, if what that thing said ... I just wanted to see her. I told her to stay off drugs. She got pissed off and kicked me out." His face screwed up slightly and he bit his lower lip a moment. "I was just trying to help. She has no idea what's coming."

"Neither do you, Ryan," Elliott said, "Like I told you, demons lie. That thing's job is to speak through that little girl and make people despair and lose hope and question their faith. As far as we know, everything it's told you has been untrue."

Sitting forward on the chair, Ryan said, "What about the guy who beat up the baby, then killed himself?"

"Like I said, the demon will mix truth with its fiction. Here." He pointed a finger to a paragraph in the book open before him and read aloud from it. "'The demon will sprinkle truth among its many lies, truths that can be proven, thus garnering the trust of the target.'" He closed the book and folded his arms across it. "You going to tell me what happened with the preacher?"

"First, the thing turned Marie on him," Ryan said. "She tried to strangle him. I had to slap her. Then the thing showed Reverend Tomlin something. I don't know what. It made him scream, and he collapsed. He had a heart attack. Marie called the hospital a little while ago. He died early this morning."

"Jeez," Elliot said as he sat back in the chair.

"What are we going to do, Mr. Granger?"

"Well, Ryan, the sad fact is, there's nothing we *can* do. I mean, we can't call the police and report a possession. In fact, if we're smart, we won't repeat this story to *anyone*. Stories like this get people labeled 'crazy.'"

Elliott's phone chirped and he picked it up. "Hello?" After several seconds, he said, "Yeah, he's here." He looked at Ryan.

"Okay, Marie, I'll do that." As he replaced the phone on its base, he said, "That was Marie. She'd like you to come home."

Ryan sighed and got up slowly.

"What's wrong?" Elliott said.

"Just wondering if she's calling me over to tell me my mom died."

"I hope not, Ryan."

After the boy was gone, Elliott went back to his books.

The sadness on Marie's face gave it away before she said a word. She served him some peach cobbler and milk at the dining room table and said, "I got a phonecall about your mother, Ryan. I'm afraid I've got some bad news for you."

He heard what she said, but at the same time, he saw the inside of that dreary little motel room. He saw Phyllis lying there on her back in her bra and panties, vomit dribbling down her cheeks. A knot tightened in his stomach.

"She OD'd, Ryan," Marie said.

Ryan stared down at his untouched cobbler. Marie reached for his hand and held it.

"I'm real sorry, Ryan," she said. "If there's anything I can do—would you like me to call the market for you? Under the circumstances, I'm sure they could find someone to work your shift today."

Ryan slowly shook his head. "No, I'll work. I want to go to work."

"All right, if that's what you want. But if you need to talk, or if you need anything at all, please let me know, will you do that?"

He nodded. "Yeah, okay."

As Ryan rode his bike to work, he let the hot summer air dry the tears from his face.

Ryan showed Karil how Kent liked the wrapped sandwiches set out on the shelf at the deli counter.

"Are you all right today, Ryan?" Karil asked as they put out the sandwiches.

He said nothing at first.

"Because you seem really sad," she said.

"I do? My mom died last night."

Karil's mouth dropped open. "What? You're mom—well, what're you doing at work?"

"I didn't know her that well," he said, but his voice trembled a little and gave him away. He had a lump in the pit of his stomach that throbbed relentlessly. "She was ... a drug addict."

"So? She was your mother, right?" Karil said. "I mean, you only get one of those. You shouldn't be working."

Kent came out from behind the deli counter and headed for the front register, but Karil stopped him.

"Kent," she said, "Ryan's mother died last night. He doesn't feel good."

Kent was a big man with silvering hair and a mustache. He turned to Ryan. "Your mother died?" he said.

Ryan nodded.

"You should've called in," Kent said. "Why don't you go on home, Ryan. You shouldn't be working."

Ryan stood with his arms down at his sides and stared at the sandwiches a moment. He chewed on his lower lip. Finally, he nodded. "Yeah. Okay. Thank you."

He took off his smock as headed for the back of the store.

From the Journal of Ryan Kettering

Even though I was expecting it, it still hurts. Not because we were close, because we weren't. Maybe it's because we weren't and we should've been. I have a gnawing ache inside me that won't go away. It's partly made of loss, partly of loneliness, and partly of fear. After talking to Maddy, all that has been combined with a huge sense of guilt. Knowing what I now know, I can see her death was my fault. I stepped into a trap.

I've never written about it, or even fully acknowledged it to myself, but I guess I've always had a fantasy tucked away in the back of my mind that Phyllis would clean herself up one day and come get me and we'd live together again, only it would be good, not like the years I lived with her before I became a ward of the state (the memories I have of those years are vague and unpleasant, like a bad dream I used to have every night when I was a kid). I guess a part of me has always clung to that fantasy. Now that she's gone, there is no hope of it ever happening. Not that there ever was, but at least while she was alive, that part of me in the very back of my mind, the part that needed that fantasy, could still hold onto that hope. Now there's not even that.

And now I've got to live with the fact that I was responsible for her death.

When I got home from work, I went to my room and did some reading. Everyone was gone, it seemed—they were at work, mostly, except for Candy and Nicole, who had to attend summer school. Lyssa worked at the nursery near Kent's Market. Marie was bustling around in the kitchen and Hank was out tending his precious garden. I left my room and headed down to the basement to watch some TV. Going down the stairs, I passed Keith coming up.

He had a strange look on his face. It was a lot like the look he'd had when I saw him leaving Maddy's room the night before— almost as if he were walking in his sleep. We bumped into each other in passing, and I said, "Hey, Keith."

He didn't say anything, just kept on going up.

At the bottom of the stairs, I turned right to go to the rec room, but heard something that made me freeze in my tracks.

"Ryan!"

It was the deep, gravelly voice that spoke through Maddy, and it was calling me from her bedroom.

"Ryan! Come here!"

I didn't want to. I wanted to go nowhere near that girl and the thing inside her.

"Come here, Ryan!"

But it sounded so urgent.

I looked into the rec room to see if anyone was there. It was empty. I turned and went down the hall to Maddy's bedroom, opened the door, and went in. I closed the door behind me.

Maddy was sitting in the chair holding a Barbie doll.

"Hello, Ryan," the voice said.

I didn't say anything.

"She didn't suffer, if that's any consolation," it said. "Of course, it never would've happened if you hadn't gone to see her."

I took a step forward. "What? What do you mean?"

"You upset her terribly," it said. "She was clean, too, and working hard on staying that way. But when you showed up with your preachy attitude, telling her to stay off drugs—well, it hurt her feelings because it made her think you didn't believe her when she told you she was clean. The thing about drug addicts, if they get upset about the tiniest little thing, first thing they want to do is get high. And they're very easily upset. You upset her. She got high. Of course, the irony is that you never would have gone over there if I hadn't told you she was going to die in the first place. And she wouldn't have died if you hadn't gone over there. Oh, what a vicious circle." It laughed, a dry, scraping laugh. "Isn't it funny how things work out?"

It laughed again. It smiled so big, Maddy's fat cheeks nearly closed her eyes as she tilted her head back and laughed. It wasn't a chuckle, it was a full, rich laugh, and it was a horrible sound, because there was no humor in it, no life. It was a non-laugh, a laugh that included none of the ingredients that make up real laughter. It was an empty sound that sent ice up and down my spine.

I lost it for a few seconds. I rushed over to Maddy and raised my fist. I was going to punch her, I really was, right in the face, as hard as I could.

"Oh, yes, that's a good way to deal with your problem," the voice said. "Beat up on a little retarded girl." It laughed some more.

I stood that way for several seconds, my arm up, my hand doubled in a fist, my lips pulled back over clenched teeth. I trembled all over. I wanted to hurt that thing. Not Maddy, but the thing inside her. I wanted to cause it great pain.

"You can't hurt me, Ryan," it said softly. "You can't touch me. I'm not a person or a thing you can harm or damage. I'm the bad things that happen to good people. I'm the unfairness in life. I'm every bit of bad luck anyone ever had. I'm not just here in this little girl, Ryan, I'm everywhere. You can't touch me. There's nothing you can do about me."

I dropped my arm and spun around, went to the door.

"Running off so soon, Ryan?" it said.

I opened the door.

"But you just got here."

It was laughing when I closed the door.

Tears stung my eyes as I hurried up the stairs. I went to the kitchen and found Marie. When she saw me, she stopped what she was doing and turned to me, and said, "Ryan, what's wrong, honey?" because I was crying, but I didn't care. I couldn't hold it back and didn't even try. She came to me and put her arms around me.

"Get rid of her, Marie," I said quietly, near Marie's ear. "You've got to get rid of her. Tell them you can't take care of her anymore, that they need to find someplace else to put her. Please, you've got to, you've *got* to."

"Oh, honey."

We stood there like that in the middle of the kitchen for awhile, Marie with her arms around me, and me bending down to put my arms around her (I'm taller than her). She said nothing for awhile, just patted me on the back gently as I cried. When she finally spoke, I wished she'd said nothing at all.

"I know it's kind of scary having her around, Ryan, but if you just ignore her, it's not so bad. Just stay away from her, that's all. It's not hard to do, since she stays in her room all the time. Just don't even think about her. And it's not all bad. The next time Dr. Sempris and the others come, Hank is going to ask for a hot tub and an SUV. Wouldn't it be nice to have a hot tub?"

I left then, and came up here to my room to write.

I'm afraid to be here, but I have nowhere else to go. I keep thinking of what the thing said—"Now that I've told you, I'll have to kill you." I don't feel safe here. I don't think Lyssa is safe, either. None of us is safe here with that thing in the basement.

I wonder if killing Maddy would get it out of the house. Why not? I'd killed my mother, why stop there? But I know I'm not going to do that. It's just something I think about. I couldn't take it out on poor Maddy.

What must she be going through, the poor girl? And there's nothing that can be done to help her.

I'm hurt and I'm angry. I feel responsible for my mother's death now, and I feel stupid for falling into the thing's trap. I want to pull all my hair out, break something, scream until I have no more voice. But I can't do any of those things, so I write.

ELEVEN

"Ryan, you can't think that way," Elliott said. "You are *not* responsible for your mother's death. She was a drug addict, and apparently, she had been for a long time. That's what happens with drug addicts, eventually they OD."

Elliott sat in his recliner. Ryan was on the couch, leaning forward with his elbows on his thighs and his face in his hands, sobbing.

"This is exactly what that thing *wants*," Elliott said. "It *wants* you to feel responsible. It wants to ruin your life, Ryan. It wants you to give up. You can't. You just can't do it. Your mother OD'd and choked to death on her own vomit. How could you *possibly* be responsible for that?"

"But if I hadn't gone over there—"

"You did that because you were *concerned* about her. You did what anyone would've done, Ryan."

Elliott said nothing for awhile and let the boy cry. Ryan rocked back and forth as he sobbed. In his silence, Elliott groped for something he could say to ease Ryan's pain, but he could think of nothing.

After his sobs subsided, Ryan got up and went to the kitchen. He got a couple papertowels and wiped his face with them, blew his nose, then sat down on the couch again.

"I don't want to live there anymore," he said. "But I've got no choice. I'm still scared that thing is going to try to kill me because I know about it."

"Look at it this way," Elliott said. "You lived there three months before you knew about it and you were fine. You've got no choice now but to put it out of your head and stay away from it. The girl stays in her room, right? So just stay away from her room. Mind your own business. You haven't told any of the others about it, have you?"

"Only Lyssa."

Elliott saw an opportunity to change the subject, which he thought needed to be done. "It sounds like you've got a great relationship with Lyssa."

Ryan smiled a little and nodded. "It is great. Lyssa means a lot to me. She's the best thing that's happened to me in a long time."

"Why don't you focus on that now," Elliott said. "Cultivate that relationship. Make it a strong and healthy one."

"Would it be all right if I brought her over sometime?"

"Sure, bring over her anytime. Come over tonight after dinner and we'll watch a movie. I've got a pretty big collection of DVDs to choose from."

Ryan's smile grew a little. His eyes were still puffy and red from crying, but he'd stopped rocking back and forth on the couch. He had, at least, pulled himself together again.

"I think we'll do that," Ryan said.

"I've got popcorn."

"Thanks, Mr. Granger. I appreciate it."

"If you're going to be hanging around, you might as well call me Elliott."

Ryan was relieved when Lyssa got home from work. They spent the rest of the day together, and Ryan told her everything that had happened that day, paying particular attention to what the thing had said about his mother's death. He felt like crying again as he talked, but he'd cried himself out over at Elliott's house. She listened and held his hand, held him. At dinner, they sat side by side at the long table in the dining room. After dinner, Ryan asked Marie for permission for the two of them to go over to Elliott's and watch a movie, and she said yes.

Ryan introduced Lyssa to Elliott.

"Elliott's a famous writer," Ryan said.

"Not that famous, I'm afraid."

Ryan said, "You're a lot more famous than I am."

Elliott laughed.

Ryan made two bags of microwave popcorn—one for Elliott,

one for himself and Lyssa—and told Lyssa to choose a movie from one of the shelves in a cabinet beside the television. She had never seen *Alien*, so they watched that and ate popcorn. After the movie, they watched some of the extras on the DVD and finished the popcorn.

Ryan did not want to go home. It no longer felt like home.

For three months, he had enjoyed living in the Preston house. He had concluded that Hank and Marie were good, decent people, and he got along with the others in the home. Best of all, he'd met Lyssa. He should've known then it was too good to be true. Now it all looked and felt different. Hank and Marie happily allowed that thing to live in their basement in exchange for swimming pools and television sets and maybe an SUV. Now, the Prestons looked as twisted and corrupt as everyone else. And now, Ryan did not feel comfortable in the house knowing that thing was always downstairs, knowing it could watch him whenever it wanted to. That thing that tricked him into killing his mother. He knew Elliott was right, that he shouldn't think that way and drive himself crazy over something he couldn't possibly have helped, but he was finding it hard to shake the fact that he'd been tricked into killing his mother. Being with Lyssa helped. Lyssa was good and decent, he had no doubt about that, and if she were with him, then he couldn't be all bad. She saw *something* good in him.

They walked very slowly from Elliott's house, hands joined between them.

"I don't want to go back in there," Ryan said.

"Then let's not."

He smiled. "Where would we go?"

"We'll go into Redding and get a hotel room. We'll order room service and watch the dirty movies."

"I wish."

"When are you going to let me read your stories, Ryan?"

"You really want to?"

"Yes."

"You don't mind that they're written by hand?"

"I can read your handwriting, I'm sure."

"Don't be. Okay. I'll bring you some tonight."

"When do you want to meet?" Lyssa said as they neared the house.

"A little later tonight. I'm tired and I think I'll get some sleep first. I'll set my watch for three, is that okay?"

"Three o'clock in the rec room."

Inside, they went down to the rec room and played some games, until Marie came down and told them it was time to clear out and get ready for bed. While everyone was going upstairs to bed, Ryan and Lyssa ducked into the laundry room off the kitchen and kissed.

"I'll see you at three," Ryan said.

"All right."

They kissed again, then headed upstairs. When he went to bed, Ryan set the alarm on his wristwatch for three o'clock. He fell asleep less than a minute after putting his head on the pillow.

It was the last time he ever saw her.

Ryan awoke with a gasp. Something loud had startled him from sleep, something much louder than the alarm on his wristwatch. He was awake instantly, pulled completely from sleep in a heartbeat. He heard the sound again.

Bam! Then, a moment later. *Bam! Bam!*

Gary was on his feet. "Did you hear that?"

"It came from the attic," Ryan said as he clambered out of his bed and stood.

"Those were gunshots," Gary said.

Ryan looked at the bed beneath Gary's bunk—it was empty.

"Where's Keith?" Gary said.

In a fraction of a second, Ryan flashed on Keith coming out of Maddy's bedroom, on Keith coming up the basement stairs with that funny distant look on his face.

"Oh, my God, Lyssa," Ryan said as he ran from the room wearing only his boxer shorts. He rushed down the hall and pressed his back against the wall beside the attic stairs when he heard someone coming down them.

The instant Keith stepped out of the narrow stairwell, gun in hand, Ryan jumped on him. Keith was bigger, but Ryan had caught him by surprise and he went down. But as soon as he hit the floor, Keith flailed and kicked and, before Ryan knew it, he'd been knocked off and was lying on the floor. Ryan scrambled to his feet, but as clumsy as he was, Keith was faster. He pointed his gun at Ryan and fired.

Ryan went down as if kicked hard in the stomach, but he remained conscious as he lay on the floor in the hall. In great pain and bleeding from the wound in his abdomen, he watched as Gary came out of the bedroom and Keith spun around, aimed the gun, and fired. He saw the hole appear in Gary's face just before he went down.

Then, without hesitating for a second, Keith put the gun in his own mouth and pulled the trigger. Ryan saw it happen in profile. He saw the splash of blood from Keith's nostrils and the spray from the back of his head half an instant before he dropped to his knees, then fell forward.

One thought repeated itself in Ryan's mind: *Lyssa ... Lyssa ... Lyssa ...*

He tried to sit up, but found he could not move his legs.

Lyssa ... Lyssa ... Lyssa ...

Ryan closed his eyes. He heard Marie scream before he slipped away.

Lyssa ...

Elliott was lying in bed trying to sleep when he heard the gunshots. They sounded very close—like they came from right next door. He heard another, then a couple more. He winced with pain as he slowly swung his legs over the edge of the bed and sat up. He turned on the lamp on the bedstand and picked up his phone. He heard a scream—it sounded like it might be Marie. He called 911.

He gave the female operator his address. "I just heard gunshots and a scream from, I think they were from the house next door."

"Do you know the people next door?"

"Yes, it's a foster-care group home. I heard seven shots."

"When did this occur?"

"Just now, just seconds ago."

"What is the address of this group home?"

He answered that and a few more questions, then the operator told him, "A unit is on the way, sir."

After he hung up, he stood and decided he might as well get up since he'd been unable to get to sleep, anyway. He slipped his robe on, pushed his walker to the kitchen, turned on the light, and put a kettle of water on the stove to boil. In the living room, he went to one of the side windows that faced the Preston house, pulled the curtain aside, and looked out. He saw nothing, but he had a bad feeling.

He put an Oscar Peterson CD into the player and turned it on. He took the book he was reading from the endtable by the recliner to the kitchen table.

By the time the water started to boil, Elliott heard the sirens drawing closer. He could hear them from all the way down on the river, and they got louder as they came up Airport Road. They didn't often come down Fig Tree, so it seemed odd when they got even louder.

He poured water into his mug, then went to the side window again and looked out. Two police cars with lights flashing were parked in front of the Preston house and officers were at the door.

Elliott cursed his temporary disability. Normally, he would go over there and see what was wrong, but not with his walker, or even with crutches—he didn't want to hobble around out there in the dark and risk falling and breaking his good hip.

He took the phone from beside his recliner to the kitchen table and called Marie's number. It rang several times, then the answering machine picked up.

"Hi, Marie, it's Elliott Granger. I just wanted to find out what's going on over there and see if there was anything I could do to help." He waited a moment, hoping someone would pick up, but no one did. "Please give me a call when you get a chance." He punched the Off button and set the phone on the table.

Elliott sighed and tried to do some reading. He was in the middle of a collection of short stories by Richard Matheson. But he couldn't concentrate. He took the teabag out of the mug and tossed it under the sink into the garbage can, and sipped his jasmine tea.

He heard another siren coming. And another. They were

closing in fast. Elliott got up and went to the window again. Two ambulances raced down Fig Tree and stopped at the Preston house. They backed up to the front yard.

"Oh, my God," Elliott muttered. He was worried about Ryan and Lyssa.

Seven shots. Nine people living in the house. Elliott wondered who had shot whom.

He went to his recliner, took the crutch leaning against it, and left the walker behind as he hobbled painfully into the kitchen and got his tea. He brought it back to the living room and put it on the endtable beside the recliner, then sat down. He turned on the lamp, turned off the music. He switched on the television and channel-surfed for awhile before getting up and going to the window again.

Four paramedics carried two bodies out of the house on stretchers—the bodies' faces were covered.

"Oh, no," Elliott breathed.

He went back to his recliner and sat down again, reclined.

Mona, his chubby dilute calico manx hopped up onto the broad armrest of his recliner. The cat sat on her haunches and faced him, meowed once.

"Hello, Mona, darlin'," he said as he stroked her back.

The cat locked Elliott's gaze with her large golden eyes and said, "You couldn't mind your own fucking business, could you?"

Elliott's entire body jerked in the chair, as if he'd been shocked. Mona's mouth had moved, and out of it had come the deep, rough, whisky voice he'd heard on the tapes Ryan had recorded.

Mona held his eyes.

"In a way, you're the cause of all this, you know," the cat said. "If you would have laughed off the boy's story in the first place, like a normal person, maybe none of this would have happened."

Cold hands closed on Elliott's throat and squeezed. Elliott clawed at his throat, but there was nothing there.

"But no, you had to encourage him. You had to give him a little James Bond tape recorder."

Elliott could not breathe. He tried to sit up, kicked his legs, flailed in his chair.

"Now you know too much. You, Ryan, and the girl. To be on

the safe side, I just killed all the kids over there. And now I'm here to kill you."

Tiny spots began to speckle Elliott's vision. He felt as if his tongue were twice its normal size. His heart throbbed in his ears as the room darkened.

"For what it's worth, Mr. Granger," the voice said, "I didn't lie about my involvement with the government. I know you were curious about that, so I thought I'd let you know. It's so frustrating to die with unanswered questions weighing on your mind."

A second before he lost consciousness and then died, Elliot heard Mona meow.

From the Journal of Ryan Kettering

It's been fourteen months since I've written in this journal. I was in the hospital some of that time. When Keith shot me, the bullet went right through me without hitting any major organs, but it knicked my spine on the way out, and now I'm paralyzed from the waist down. I had to have a couple operations, and then a lot of physical therapy, but it didn't do any good because I'm still in this fucking chair.

No one ever figured out where Keith got the gun. I was the only one who survived. Keith killed all the others and himself. Except, of course, for Hank and Marie. Keith didn't go after them. Or Maddy. He left her alone. But that only makes sense because it was Maddy—it was the thing *inside* Maddy—that made Keith do it. I have no doubt of that. Keith was as pliable as Play-Doh. If he'd do anything Gary told him to, then how easy would it be for that *thing* to bend him to its will?

It killed Lyssa.

That's been the hardest part of all to get over. I still haven't. I never will. When I found out Lyssa was dead, I was sorry Keith's bullet hadn't killed me.

It killed Mr. Granger, too. The official cause was a heart attack, but I know better. He knew too much. I felt like that was my fault. If I hadn't involved him—

But then, this was *ALL* my fault. I involved Lyssa, I involved Mr. Granger, I involved Reverend Tomlin. This was all my fault.

While I was in the hospital, my social worker, Annie Kintner, came to see me.

"I want to be transferred to another home," I told her.

"That's understandable. I'm going to see what I can do, okay?"

"You promise?"

"I promise I'll try, but I can't promise results, Ryan, you know that."

"I want a new place by the time I get out of the hospital."

"I'll see what I can do," Annie said.

But she hadn't seen well enough, because when I got out of the hospital, I was brought back here to the Preston house. It was unrecognizable, though. It had been completely remodeled inside. There was also an SUV parked in the driveway.

"And look at this, Ryan," Marie said as she wheeled my chair to the stairs. A chair-lift had been installed on the staircase. "There's one on the basement stairs, too. The entire house has been made handicapped-friendly. Isn't that nice? Dr. Sempris and her colleagues did this especially for you. You're going to be our only foster child, Ryan. For awhile, anyway. Well, you and ... and Maddy, of course." She leaned forward and whispered in my ear, "Things will be okay, I promise."

The day after I got home from the hospital, one of the black Lexus sedans came to the house and the white-haired woman with glasses, Dr. Sempris, came in. She asked to see me in the dining room. Marie set us up with coffee and apple pie.

"I'm Dr. Sempris, Ryan, and I'm going to explain the situation to you," she said. "I know you want to be transfered out of this house, but Maddy wants you to stay."

"*Maddy* wants me to stay?" I said.

"Yes, Maddy. The little girl. She likes you. She wants you to stay and she wants you to come visit her."

"No way. I will not listen to that thing anymore. I won't—"

"You won't have to. It will leave you alone if you will agree to visit with Maddy for awhile every day."

"You're kidding, right?" I really didn't believe her. It sounded like some kind of trick.

"I'm not. I'll be honest, Ryan, it's in our best interest to keep Maddy as happy and healthy as possible. She likes you. The presence will leave you alone during these periods. You have my guarantee."

"That means I have to stay here."

"Yes."

"I don't want to stay here."

"I think we can come to an understanding. In exchange for your daily visits with Maddy, Ryan, we are prepared to set you up with a top-of-the-line computer, with all the accessories. We will find a writer to work with you, to tutor you in writing. And lastly, I will personally set you up with a New York literary agent who will turn you into the writer you've always wanted to be. And on top of all that, you get to stay here as long as you like, and you and Maddy will be the only ones here, so Marie and Hank can give you their full attention."

"What's the alternative?" I said.

"There is no alternative, Ryan," Dr. Sempris said. "Do you understand?"

"*No* alternative?"

The corners of Dr. Sempris's mouth curled up in a cold approximation of a smile. "Let's be honest with each other, Mr. Kettering. You are alive right now only by accident. I think you understand that. It was an accident that very easily could be rectified, if the presence saw fit to do so. We are offering you an opportunity to be useful for us, and in return, we shall be useful to you."

Like I said before, foster care is like playing Russian roulette. Sometimes the hammer clicks and you're fine, and sometimes you take a bullet to the brain.

I've taken enough bullets lately.

I visit with Maddy every day. Sometimes we just talk, and other times we play with her dolls together. Sometimes we go to the rec room and watch TV or play video games.

The thing has never spoken up once. I know it's there, and that really bothered me for awhile, at first. But the longer I went without hearing its voice, the easier it was not to think about it while I was with Maddy.

She really is a sweet, good-natured girl. She doesn't talk about the thing, or where she goes when it comes forward. She doesn't complain.

It's a great place to live, and Marie was right—the whole house had been made handicapped-friendly. There were even rails on the hot tub that allowed me to lower myself in and pull myself out.

They come every few weeks, the people Marie had called the "dentist people," and they spend hours in Maddy's bedroom with her. Fortunately, they usually come while I'm in school so I don't have to see them. They were still here when Marie drove me home from school one day a couple weeks ago. I usually try to avoid them, but I caught Dr. Sempris in the downstairs hallway.

"Are things going well, Ryan?" she said.

"Yes. Things are fine."

"You're happy?"

"Yes, I'm happy."

"You're not smiling."

"I'm sorry, but as happy as I am, I don't smile that much anymore."

"You've had no problem with the presence?"

The presence. For a few seconds, I didn't know what she was talking about. I never thought of it of as *the presence.* And I guess I just don't think about it that much anymore, period.

"No," I said, "I haven't."

She smiled and said, "That's good. I'm glad."

I took a couple folded-together sheets of paper from my back pocket and handed them over to Dr. Sempris.

"What's this?" she said.

"It's a list of all the movies I want on DVD. Widescreen only, no full-frames."

She unfolded the pages and her eyes scanned the columns of titles. When she looked at me, her right eyebrow arched high above her eye. "I don't think this will be a problem, Ryan."

"Good," I said. "Thank you." I turned and went upstairs to my room.

My literary agent, Liz Rosenstein, has read my short stories and says I'm good. She's encouraging me to write a novel about a character in one of my stories. She's going to send a writer to work with me until I get the hang of writing a novel. She thinks she can make a big splash with me as some kind of boy genius.

Marie and Hank remain the same. Except for one thing—Marie doesn't go to church anymore.

About the Author

Ray Garton is the author of sixty books, including horror novels such as the Bram Stoker Award–nominated *Live Girls*, *Crucifax*, *Lot Lizards*, and *The Loveliest Dead*; thrillers like *Sex and Violence in Hollywood*, *Murder Was My Alibi*, and *Trade Secrets*; and seven short story collections. He has also written several movie and TV tie-ins and a number of young adult novels under the name Joseph Locke. In 2006, he received the Grand Master of Horror Award. He lives in northern California with his wife.

OPEN ROAD
INTEGRATED MEDIA

Open Road Integrated Media is a digital publisher and multimedia content company. Open Road creates connections between authors and their audiences by marketing its ebooks through a new proprietary online platform, which uses premium video content and social media.

Videos, Archival Documents, and New Releases

Sign up for the Open Road Media newsletter and get news delivered straight to your inbox.

Sign up now at
www.openroadmedia.com/newsletters

FIND OUT MORE AT
WWW.OPENROADMEDIA.COM

FOLLOW US:
@openroadmedia and
Facebook.com/OpenRoadMedia

CPSIA information can be obtained
at www.ICGtesting.com
Printed in the USA
JSHW042025310122
22449JS00001B/99

9 781497 642645